Mary Anne and the Zoo Mystery

Other books by
Ann M. Martin

Rachel Parker, Kindergarten Show-off

Eleven Kids, One Summer

Ma and Pa Dracula

Yours Turly, Shirley

Ten Kids, No Pets

Slam Book

Just a Summer Romance

Missing Since Monday

With You and Without You

Me and Katie (the Pest)

Stage Fright

Inside Out

Bummer Summer

BABY-SITTERS LITTLE SISTER series

THE BABY-SITTERS CLUB mysteries

THE BABY-SITTERS CLUB series

Mary Anne and the Zoo Mystery
Ann M. Martin

AN
APPLE
PAPERBACK

SCHOLASTIC INC.
New York Toronto London Auckland Sydney

Cover art by Hodges Soileau

No part of this publication may be reproduced in whole or in part, or stored in a retrieval system, or transmitted in any form or by any means, electronic, mechanical, photocopying, recording, or otherwise, without written permission of the publisher. For information regarding permission, write to Scholastic Inc., 555 Broadway, New York, NY 10012.

ISBN 0-590-48309-9

12 11 10 9 8 7 6 5 4 3 2 1   5 6 7 8 9/9 0/0

Printed in the U.S.A.   40

First Scholastic printing, April 1995

*The author gratefully acknowledges
Jahnna Beecham and Malcolm Hilgartner
for their help in
preparing this manuscript.*

CHAPTER 1

"Listen to this! Bedford Zoo to host animal world VIPs." I held up the front page of the newspaper, which displayed a large color photo. "James and Mojo."

"Mojo?" a voice from the kitchen door repeated. "What kind of a name is that?"

I giggled. "It's a name for a gorilla." I turned the newspaper so Dawn could see. "Here's her picture. Isn't she darling?"

"Mary Anne, you think every fuzzy-faced, four-legged creature is darling," Dawn said.

I thought about it — but not for long. "I guess I do." As if to prove it, I picked up my extremely cute gray-striped kitten off the floor and plopped him in my lap. "Isn't that right, Tigger?"

Tigger's motor started instantly. I scratched him in one of his favorite spots, between the ears, and smiled as his eyelids dropped to half-mast.

Since you've already met Tigger and Dawn, I guess I should introduce myself. I'm Mary Anne Spier. I'm thirteen years old, and I live in Stoneybrook, Connecticut, with my dad, my stepmother Sharon, and my stepsister Dawn (and Tigger).

You'll notice I said stepmother and stepsister. That's because this is my dad's second marriage. He didn't get divorced, like a lot of parents I know. My mother died when I was a baby, so I have no memories of her. We have photos of her, so I know what she looked like, but it's not quite the same as remembering.

For the longest time, it was just me and my father. Because he had to raise me all by himself, Dad used to be really strict. I'm not kidding. For one thing, I couldn't talk on the phone, except to ask questions about homework. But the worst thing was the way he made me dress. Can you imagine a seventh-grader wearing pigtails and jumpers with kneesocks? It was terrible. I felt like a baby.

To make matters worse, I was — and still am — extremely shy. It was difficult for me to make friends. It was also hard for me to stand up to my father. When I finally did, it really changed my life.

This is how it happened. I'm a member of the Baby-sitters Club (which I'll tell you more

2

about later), or the BSC. Through the BSC, I had taken a job baby-sitting for Jenny Prezzioso, a three-year-old. After her parents left for the afternoon, Jenny got really sick. She had a fever of one hundred and four degrees. I couldn't reach her parents so I called all of the numbers the Prezziosos had left for me, but no one was home. Finally I called 911. The operator sent an ambulance right away and we took Jenny to the hospital.

It was a very scary experience, but Dad was impressed with my responsible behavior. That gave me the courage to talk to him about being allowed to grow up.

Now I dress the way I want, which is still pretty conservative. I mean, I wear the latest styles and all, but I don't go overboard. My dark brown hair is no longer in pigtails. In fact, I recently had it cut short (to my chin). It's bouncy and very easy to take care of. I talk to my friends when I want to and — are you ready for this? I have a steady boyfriend, which would have been a major no-no before.

What can I tell you about Logan Bruno? He's cute (I think he looks just like my favorite star, Cam Geary), and he's charming, especially with that southern accent (Logan's from Louisville, Kentucky). He's a great athlete, an extremely nice guy, and a member of the Baby-sitters Club. Well, not a full-fledged member.

3

Logan's an associate member, which means he helps out when we have too many jobs and not enough sitters to go around.

Back to my dad. Once he realized that I didn't need to be watched so closely, he discovered that he could get on with his own life. Which was great, and that's how I ended up with this wonderful new family.

You see, it all started when I met Dawn Schafer, who had just moved to Stoneybrook with her mom and brother, Jeff. Dawn's family had been living in California, but when her mom and dad got divorced, Sharon (Dawn's mom) returned, with her kids, to the place where she grew up — Stoneybrook. Dawn and I quickly became friends. Then a truly amazing thing happened.

One day, Dawn and I were looking through my father's high school yearbook. We had tons of fun laughing at all of the strange hairdos and funny outfits that they wore twenty years ago. Then we saw a message he had written to S.E.P. under his picture. S.E.P. were Dawn's mother's initials before she got married! We flipped to Sharon's picture. It said "Dearest Richie" with a really gushy message signed "Always and forever, Sharon."

Richie was my dad. He and Sharon had been high school sweethearts. Isn't that incredible? Dawn and I decided that instant that we had a mission — to get Sharon and Richie back together.

We reintroduced them to each other, and love did the rest. Before we knew it they were dating, and after awhile, they married. Did we all live happily ever after? Of course!

Well, it wasn't quite that simple. You see, Dad and I moved in with Sharon and Dawn. (My ten-year-old stepbrother Jeff had already gone back to California. He had had a tough time adjusting to his new school here in Stoneybrook, plus he really missed his dad and friends back on the West Coast.)

To be honest, we all had some trouble adjusting to each other at first. You see, Dawn and Sharon are extremely casual people. They don't worry if the house gets a little messy. Or even a lot messy. Sharon is pretty absentminded, too, which adds to the clutter. She'll put her shoes in the refrigerator and the orange juice in the hall closet. After she's cooked dinner (which is usually some form of vegetarian cuisine), the kitchen can officially be declared a disaster area. Every pan and utensil is on the counter, drawers are left open, and the sink is piled high with dishes. That doesn't bother Sharon or Dawn.

But it sure bothers Dad, who is a full-fledged neat freak. My father's socks are organized by color in his dresser. His shirts are hung exactly one inch apart in his closet. His desk looks like a window display for office supplies and his car still smells new, even though it's several years old.

At first Dawn and I tried to share a room, but we soon discovered that we were just too different. She listens to music when she does her homework; I like silence. Her idea of a late snack is an apple and a carton of yogurt. For me, it's a plate full of Oreos and a tall glass of milk. When we finally set up separate rooms, life became much easier.

There have been a few other rough spots — such as when Dawn went back to California to live with her dad for awhile because she missed him so terribly. That was hard. We talked on the phone a lot (you should have seen the phone bills!), but it still wasn't the same as having her in the next room. Now Dawn is living with us again, and I'm thrilled. I don't even mind her weird granola toast and special oat-and-nuts cereal (I've even taken to eating it for breakfast myself).

In fact, when she appeared in the doorway that Saturday, half asleep and verging on being a grouch, I had already eaten a large bowl of the stuff hours earlier.

"Mojo," Dawn muttered, pushing her long blonde hair away from her face as she bent to fill her cereal bowl. "How come James got a regular name, and Mojo was stuck with Mojo? That hardly seems fair."

"They'll be at the Bedford Zoo. We have to go and see them," I declared, putting the paper down. "Since it's springtime, I'll bet lots of the animals are having babies. I can't wait to see them!"

Dawn was starting to wake up. She took a sip of the orange juice she'd poured herself. "That sounds like fun. Why don't we go to-day?"

I shook my head. "Can't. Logan's coming over and the three of us are going to a movie, downtown. Remember?"

"How are we getting there?"

"Bikes. You know that." I snapped my fingers in front of her bewildered face.

"I'm awake," Dawn insisted, slapping at her cheeks. "Really I am. It's all coming back to me. Lunch, yesterday. Logan asked us to go to a movie. We said maybe. He said he'd treat. We said definitely. I remember." Dawn shrugged and smiled. "See? My amnesia is cured."

Ding-dong!

"That must be him," I said, hopping up from the kitchen table. "I'll get it."

"What's he doing here so early?"

I pointed to the clock on the microwave. "It's one o'clock, sleepyhead."

Now Dawn was really awake. I don't think I've ever seen her move so fast. She gulped the rest of her orange juice, inhaled her cereal, and raced up the stairs to her room. Moments later she appeared dressed in a pair of jeans, a purple-and-white cotton baseball jersey, and a purple sun visor.

"Anyone want to bicycle into town with me?" she puffed, a little red-faced from all that running.

Logan wasn't fooled. He grinned. "You sound like you just ran a marathon. Maybe you ought to take a break for a few minutes before we hit the street."

"Thanks." Dawn collapsed into a chair, gasping for air. "I don't mind if I do."

Twenty minutes later, we were pedaling downtown. I just love spring in Stoneybrook. Daffodils and irises poke their heads up along the walkways of Main Street. Apple trees are in bloom, and the air smells delicious.

Summer fashions had taken over the window displays and we *ooh*ed and *ah*ed our way to the downtown cinema. We locked our bikes in the rack out front and then took our place in the ticket line, which was fairly long.

It was moving pretty slowly, too. As we passed the window of the candy store near the theater, I noticed an unusual poster. It was a picture of a very sad-looking elephant.

Prison bars had been drawn across his face.

" 'Free Babar,' " I read out loud. "Did you see this, Logan?"

He and Dawn stood next to me, reading the poster.

"Poor little elephant. Imagine being stuck in a cage at the Valley Park Shopping Center," I said.

"Where's that?" Logan asked.

"Near Stamford," I replied. "They bought the elephant from a circus, and are using him to promote the shopping center. This is awful. The poor thing doesn't have any room to move around."

Little Babar looked so sad peering out from behind the prison bars. I could feel my eyes filling with tears. (Did I mention that I am very emotional?)

"Uh-oh. Find your handkerchiefs." Dawn groaned. "Mary Anne's going to cry."

Logan, who is used to seeing me cry at television commercials, patted my arm. "Don't get all worked up. Babar will be okay."

"That's right," Dawn added, pointing to the bottom of the poster. "See? They're taking up a collection to raise money to move him to a real zoo."

Now my vision was definitely blurred. (Once I start, it's hard to stop.) I dug in my purse for some money. "I'll give Babar something. Here's a dollar and thirty-three cents."

Logan held a dollar bill in the air. "I'll chip in a dollar."

Dawn emptied her entire coin purse in the palm of my hand. "That's all I can find. But Babar can have it."

As the movie line pushed forward, I stepped out. I raced inside the candy store and found a small can marked, *Money for Babar*, sitting on the counter beside the cash register. I stuffed in the dollars and change as fast as I could, then hurried to join my friends, who had just reached the ticket window.

"Feel better?" Logan asked as he handed us our movie tickets.

I nodded. "A little. But I'd feel a lot better if I knew Babar was leaving that awful place."

We found three seats in the middle of the theater. Logan, great guy that he is, bought popcorn and soft drinks for Dawn and me. Soon the lights went down and the opening credits began to roll. It was hard to concentrate on the movie, though. All I could think of was that sad little elephant's face. I knew I wanted to do more than drop a few coins in a can, and hope for the best. But what?

The Baby-sitters Club! Of course! We could make freeing Babar a club effort. It would be a great community service and our charges

10

would love it. I decided to talk to the members of the BSC on Monday.

I tossed another big handful of popcorn in my mouth and leaned back comfortably in my seat. When Logan took my hand and gave it a squeeze, I gave him a big smile. Now that I'd come up with a way to help free Babar, I could finally enjoy the movie.

CHAPTER 2

"He kind of looks like Dumbo," Claudia Kishi said, examining the elephant's photograph.

It was Monday afternoon and I had brought a Free Babar poster to our Baby-sitters Club meeting to show the rest of the members.

Kristy Thomas, our club president and my other best friend, jumped on the idea. "The BSC could do a lot to help free Babar," she said, leaning back in the director's chair that she always sits in during club meetings. "If you guys want, we can organize the kids and help spread the word. Maybe we can even do a few projects to help raise money for Babar."

I love it when Kristy gets excited about a project. She puts herself one hundred percent behind it and makes it happen.

Take the Baby-sitters Club, one of her greatest ideas of all time. She came up with the idea to form the club while sitting in her

12

kitchen one day, listening to her mom try to find a baby-sitter. You see, Kristy's father walked out on her family when Kristy was six and never looked back. That left Kristy's mom to work and raise four kids. Anyway, on that afternoon last year, Mrs. Thomas (that was her name then) made phone call after phone call trying to find someone to take care of David Michael, Kristy's younger brother (he's seven and a half now).

That's when the great idea hit Kristy like a bolt out of the blue.

Why not form a club consisting of responsible, experienced sitters? Parents could make one call, to the club, and reach a whole bunch of good sitters at once. Brilliant, huh?

In the beginning, there were only four of us — me, Kristy, Claudia, and Stacey McGill. Claudia, who is a fantastic artist, designed our fliers and the club was on its way. We decided to meet three times a week, on Mondays, Wednesdays, and Fridays from five-thirty to six in Claud's room.

Kristy and I used to live across the street from Claudia on Bradford Court. That's all changed now. I already told you that my dad married Sharon and we moved into their farmhouse. Well, Kristy's mom married Watson Brewer (a genuine millionaire) and Kristy and her three brothers — Charlie, age seventeen,

Sam, age fifteen, and David Michael — moved into his big beautiful mansion on the other side of town.

Watson has two kids from his first marriage, seven-year-old Karen and Andrew, who's four. After he married Mrs. Thomas (now Mrs. Brewer), they adopted Emily Michelle, a two-year-old from Vietnam. Then Nannie, Kristy's grandmother, moved in to help look after everybody. When Karen and Andrew are living at the big house (they call their mom's house the little house), which is every other month, there are *ten* people at the Brewer mansion. It's a good thing it's so huge.

But anyway, in the beginning, when the club was formed, Kristy and Claudia and Stacey and I were neighbors. We decided to hold our meetings at Claud's because she has a phone in her room and — are you ready for this? — it's not just an extension, it's her very own phone line.

Kristy became president because the club was her idea and because she's a real leader. (Some people would say she's loud and bossy, but I prefer to call her strong-willed.) We can count on Kristy to be at every meeting in her jeans, sneakers, and a turtleneck shirt. She usually wears her baseball cap placed firmly on her brown hair, which is pulled into a ponytail.

14

Since we were holding meetings at Claudia's, we elected her vice-president. Claud does a lot of things for the club, such as pick up calls when the club's not in session and supply us with snacks. She is also our resident artist and all-around cool, creative person. In the looks category, I would say that Claudia is gorgeous with her shiny jet black hair and perfect clear complexion.

Claudia does have a couple of flaws. (Don't we all?) One, she is a major junk food addict. I'm not kidding. She stashes cookies and candy bars all over her room. And two, although she is very smart, schoolwork is Claudia's nemesis. She can paint a picture of clouds soaring over a summer landscape with her eyes closed, but ask her to diagram a sentence and she freezes up completely. At one point her parents were so concerned about her falling behind in her studies that they asked her to consider quitting the BSC. It was awful. Fortunately, Claudia pulled her grades up so she didn't have to quit. But we understand that, for Claudia, homework *has* to come first.

Stacey McGill, who is a real math whiz, was our first treasurer. She and Claudia are a lot alike. Both have the absolute coolest clothes — not because they're rich and can afford to buy a million outfits, but because they have a real sense of style.

Claudia will go to a used clothing store and buy an old black vest, a beat-up derby, and an old-fashioned collarless shirt for a few dollars. Then she'll add some lace and beads to the vest to make it extra funky. She'll make a sequined headband for the derby and belt the big white shirt over some wild leggings and *voilà!* She looks like a million dollars.

Stacey's style is just as cool, but a little more sophisticated and sleek. I think it comes from the fact that she lived in New York City for such a long time. She grew up there. Stacey also acts a little more grown-up than the rest of us because she's had to deal with some serious problems in her life, the biggest one being her diabetes. Stacey's body can't process sugar, so she has to give herself daily shots of insulin. Can you imagine sticking yourself with a needle? Ew! I just couldn't do it.

Stacey and Claudia used to be best friends. Unfortunately, Stacey's no longer in the club, which makes me sad just thinking about it. I mean, we have all been such close friends and have gone through so much together, it just doesn't feel right for her not to be in the BSC.

Here's what happened: A number of us have boyfriends. Kristy has Bart Taylor (though she would never officially call him her boyfriend). Bart is this boy in the neighborhood who coaches a softball team for kids, like

Kristy's team, the Krushers. And as I said, I have Logan. Well, Stacey's seeing this guy named Robert Brewster, but her attachment to him is different. She decided that he meant more to her than the BSC or any of our friendships did, so she quit our club. Before she did, a lot of harsh words were said by everyone, which I think we all regret. (I know I do.) But one of the things Stacey said that really sticks in my mind is that she felt we were too babyish for her. That hurt. I hope we can work it out someday, but for now, Stacey is not in the club. So Dawn, who's usually our alternate officer (that's the person who takes over the duties of an officer who can't make a meeting), is now serving as club treasurer, which she winces at because math is not her strong suit.

I was voted club secretary because I have the best handwriting in the group and because I am a very organized person. Believe me, you have to be organized in order to do this job. You see, I keep track of everyone's schedules — when they go to ballet class, or a French club meeting, or to the orthodontist. I know when Kristy's Krushers hold their practices, and when Claudia's art class has an exhibition.

Besides knowing all of our personal schedules, I schedule every single baby-sitting job. When a client calls, we jot down the important information — who, when, where, how many children, and so on — and then I check the record book to see which of our club members is free. If the record book were wrong, things could get pretty crazy. This may sound like bragging, but I'm proud to say that I have never made a mistake.

Mallory Pike and Jessica Ramsey joined our club later and are the BSC's junior officers. We call them that because they are eleven and in the sixth grade, and they're not allowed to baby-sit at night, except for their own families.

Besides being best friends, they are totally horse crazy. They love horse movies, *The Black Stallion* and *Black Beauty* being among their favorites, and horse books, especially the ones written by Marguerite Henry. Neither of them has ever owned a horse, but they dream about it.

Both girls have special talents and big dreams for the future. Mal would like to be a children's book author and illustrator someday. (She's off to a good start, too, having won best all-around fiction for the sixth grade on Young Authors' Day.) Jessi, with her beautiful long legs and graceful body, is a ballet dancer. She's danced leading roles in several productions and hopes to dance with a major company like the New York City Ballet one day. I'm certain she'll do it, too.

Though they have a lot in common, Jessi

and Mal are also very different. First of all, Jessi is black and Mallory is white. Jessi has two siblings: Becca, who's eight and a half, and her baby brother Squirt (his real name, John Philip Ramsey, Jr., is awfully big for such a little guy).

Mallory has *seven* brothers and sisters. Mallory is the oldest (she's eleven), followed by the triplets, Byron, Adam, and Jordan, who are ten. Then comes nine-year-old Vanessa, eight-year-old Nicky, Margo, who's seven, and last, but certainly not least, five-year-old Claire. They all have reddish-brown hair and blue eyes, and three of them — Mallory, Vanessa, and Nicky — wear glasses. (Mal longs to trade in her frames for a pair of contacts, but her parents say she has to wait until she's older.)

I think I've covered everyone except Shannon Kilbourne, who has taken over Dawn's old job of alternate officer. Shannon lives across the street from Kristy. When those two first met, they didn't like each other *at all*. Kristy thought Shannon was a big snob, but it was all a misunderstanding. Kristy soon found out that Shannon was very nice, and that she was also a great baby-sitter. She invited Shannon to become an associate member of the BSC, like Logan. Despite her heavy involvement with activities at her school, Shannon has been doing a lot of filling in lately — first, when Dawn was in California, and now, with Stacey out of the club.

Speaking of Stacey, Claudia and Dawn were having a pretty intense discussion about her. I don't know how they got from Babar to Stacey and Robert, but in the course of a half hour we usually manage to talk about lots of things, as well as take calls from clients, which is our main reason for meeting.

"Oh, Stacey saw me, all right," Dawn was saying. "She started to wave but then she looked away really fast."

Kristy looked cross. "I guess we should probably think about a permanent replacement."

"Oh, not yet," Claudia pleaded. "Let's give it a little more time. I mean, we're okay, aren't we?"

Everyone looked at me, probably because I'm the one who does the scheduling. "We're fine," I said. "Especially since Shannon has made herself available to help out more. She doesn't get to every meeting, but she gets to most of them."

Shannon gave us a reassuring smile. "I'm here whenever you need me."

There was a collective sigh of relief. None of us even wanted to think about replacing Stacey. It was too uncomfortable.

20

"Okay!" Kristy clapped her hands together. "Back to Babar. Why don't we talk to our charges about the Babar campaign this week? Find out if they're interested."

"Why don't we do a survey?" I suggested. "I could divide up the client list in no time."

Kristy gave me a thumbs-up sign. I pulled some paper out of the back of the record book, and started writing furiously.

"I've got a ton of schoolwork tonight," Claudia said with a moan, gesturing to the stack of books on her desk. "My calls may have to wait till tomorrow."

"Speaking of school," Dawn said, "have you guys noticed anything about the science teachers?"

I nodded. "Every time I see Mrs. Gonzalez, she's talking in some corner with Ms. Griswold, looking all excited."

"They've been hinting for weeks about some biology project that's in the works," Kristy said. "And this morning I heard Mrs. Gonzalez say Wednesday's the day."

"Do you think they're going to make some kind of announcement?" I asked.

"Yup," Kristy said, tugging on the visor of her favorite cap. (It has a picture of a collie on it.) "There's supposed to be a presentation for the eighth-graders."

Claudia hit her head with the palm of her

hand. "That explains why Ms. Griswold was in the art room picking up posterboard and paints. She said she had some large photos that needed mounting. She also mentioned something about a slide show."

"Maybe they're planning a trip," Dawn said excitedly, "to someplace cool, like Woods Hole, where they study the whales."

"Or maybe they've decided that dissecting frogs isn't enough," Kristy said mysteriously. "Maybe they're going to have us operate on muskrats or groundhogs."

"Ew! Gross!" everyone squealed at once.

Mallory and Jessi exchanged worried looks. "I'm not looking forward to biology one bit," Mal whispered.

"Kristy's just kidding," I said, patting Mallory on the arm. "Don't worry. We don't have to dissect anything if we don't want to."

Shannon folded her arms grumpily. "Gee, at my school, all we do is stare at swamp water through a microscope. We're studying the life cycle of a paramecium. I'd give anything for some exciting new project, like operating on groundhogs."

That prompted another round of ews! Luckily a client called, putting an end to discussing gross operations.

The phone seemed to ring nonstop for the next fifteen minutes. I was so busy writing in the record book that I barely had time to make out the contact sheets for the Free Babar campaign. But I finished them just as the digital clock on Claud's desk turned from five-fifty-nine to six o'clock.

Kristy, efficient leader that she is, checked the clock and announced, "This meeting of the Baby-sitters Club is officially over."

CHAPTER 3

Wednesday was the day the biology project was to be revealed. Even kids who couldn't stand science were excited.

"Have you seen what's in the front office?" Kristy called to Dawn and me as we arrived for school that morning. "It's a huge box with signs all over it that say *Top Secret*."

A lot of kids had gathered outside the doors to the office and were peering in, speculating on what might be inside the box.

"It's a car," declared Alan Gray (who is our class goof-off).

Claudia, who was standing next to him, rolled her eyes and said, "It's for biology class, remember?"

"Okay, so it's not a car. It's a Jeep. For exploring the jungle."

Howie Johnson punched him on the shoulder. "Yeah, like there are sooooo many jungles in Connecticut."

"Can it," Kristy ordered in her best coach voice. "Or you're going to miss the next event."

"Event?" Alan squinted one eye shut and stared at Kristy as if she were crazy.

Kristy simply pointed at the parking lot, where a dark car was pulling in. Three people dressed in trench coats, felt slouch hats, and dark glasses got out of the car just as loud music began blasting from the school's speakers. The tape was old, and it crackled as the singer wailed, "Secret agent man, secret agent man."

"That's Ms. Griswold," Dawn declared. "With Ms. Harris and Mrs. Gonzalez."

The entire science department had come to school in costume. We followed them into the building and watched as they pushed the huge brown box toward the SMS auditorium. The box was on wheels so it moved easily. Just before it disappeared through the auditorium's double doors, I swear I saw the box jump.

"Did you see that?" I whispered to Dawn.

She nodded excitedly. "I think whatever's in that box is — " She turned and raised her hands above her head, making a monster face. "*Alive!*"

"Frankenstein," Alan Gray's voice bellowed over the crowd. "They've created a monster and we're going to have to take care of it."

"A horse," Brent Jensen announced.

"Yeah, dream on," Todd Long replied.

The bell rang, interrupting the chatter. For the first time that I can remember, the halls cleared almost instantly. Students were actually anxious for school to start, so we could find out what was in that box.

My locker (number thirty-two) is about as far away from homeroom as you can get. I tossed my school books inside and then Dawn and I raced for Mr. Blake's classroom.

Moments after Mr. Blake took attendance, the PA system crackled to life.

"Good morning, students," the voice of our principal said pleasantly.

"Good morning, Mr. Taylor," a few of the boys in the rear of the room shouted back in a singsong voice. Mr. Blake silenced them with a stern look.

"You may be wondering about the large package that was in the front hall. It came by special delivery this morning and has been making strange sounds ever since."

"I was forced to call the authorities," Mr. Taylor continued. "And, luckily for SMS, three special agents were dispatched immediately. They have surrounded the package in question and have moved it to the auditorium. Upon closer examination, they discovered its contents were bigger than any of them had ex-

26

pected. Special Agent Harris just spoke to me and said she was going to need the help of the entire eighth grade."

"All right!" Alan Gray gave Justin Forbes a high-five. "We get out of class."

The loudspeaker crackled again. "Teachers, when I announce your name, please have your students proceed in an orderly manner to the auditorium."

Mr. Taylor read off the names of several other teachers before Mr. Blake's name was called.

Dawn and I led the class to the auditorium. As we filed in, I looked for the rest of the eighth-grade BSC members. Kristy was in front with her homeroom, and I spotted Claudia's red sequined baseball cap in the middle of the auditorium. Logan's class was behind Claudia's. He had turned in his seat and was looking for me. We made eye contact and waved. Then Dawn and I led our group to our seats on the left side of the auditorium.

Onstage, Ms. Griswold and Ms. Harris, who were still in their trench coats, stood guard in front of the mysterious box. Several large easels draped in red cloth lined the stage. Mrs. Gonzalez was at the podium.

"Boy, this project must be a really big deal," I whispered to Dawn. "Look at how much work they put into the presentation."

27

When everyone was seated, the lights dimmed and a recording of roaring lions and jungle sounds filled the air. Then a movie was projected onto a screen.

"The hidden lives of animals," the deep voice of the narrator announced.

For the next ten minutes we watched different kinds of animals doing the craziest things. One sequence I especially liked showed a family of shrews (which are like tiny moles) taking a walk. The mother went first, with all the babies following along behind, each holding onto the tail of the one in front. They reminded me of a group of preschoolers taking a trip to the park.

When the film clip ended, Mrs. Gonzalez tightened the belt on her trench coat, then said, "Perhaps you're wondering why we called you here."

She moved to one of the easels and whipped off the red cloth, revealing a picture of a giraffe. Underneath the photo were printed the words, *I've got a secret.*

Ms. Harris moved to her easel and revealed a picture of a tiger with the same message. "I've got a secret."

Ms. Griswold's easel had a picture of a grizzly bear, and another held an ostrich.

"All of these animals lead secret lives," Mrs. Gonzalez said. "Your mission is to choose one

28

animal, any kind of animal, and observe and record every action it makes. I want you to find out what it eats and when it eats it. How it walks. What makes it happy. What it does for fun. When it naps. Everything. And then report back to us—" (she gestured to her colleagues) " — in three weeks."

Erica Blumberg, who is in my homeroom, raised her hand. "But where are we going to find these animals? I don't have a pet. How can I observe any animal that closely?"

"I'm glad you asked that question, Erica," Mrs. Gonzalez said with a grin. "That brings me to part two of our presentation. Stoneybrook Middle School has gone into partnership with another institution. Ready, teachers?"

They nodded.

"Hit it!"

The teachers opened their trench coats to reveal brightly colored T-shirts underneath. On the front was a design of a kid in a trench coat examining a toucan with a huge magnifying glass. Printed across the bottom of the shirt was the slogan, *The best kept secret in Connecticut.*

The teachers turned around in unison. Across the backs of their shirts were the words, *Bedford Zoo.*

"Bedford Zoo has become our partner," Mrs. Gonzalez said. "For the next three weeks, special buses will be waiting in the parking lot after school to take SMS students to the zoo. You can either study a pet at home or choose an animal at the zoo. Whatever you choose, it's important to remember that your report must be based solely on observation. No textbooks of any sort are allowed. The student with the best researched project will win a prize."

"A prize?" Alan Gray cried. "Is it in that box?"

"No, the prize wouldn't fit in there," Mrs. Gonzalez replied, laughing. "But what's in our box is the reason we're so excited about this biology project. Ms. Griswold, will you do the honors?"

"I'd be delighted." Ms. Griswold moved to the box and unfastened some metal clasps on one side. Before she opened it, though, she turned and cautioned us to be quiet. "What I have in here is very sensitive. She's a little afraid of crowds and definitely bothered by loud noises. So I'll need your cooperation to make her feel safe and comfortable. Would all of you welcome — gently — our newest student?"

I could feel goosebumps creep up my arm as she opened the box. Inside was a metal cage, and sitting inside that, clutching a baby doll, was a chimpanzee.

"Awww!"

"She is so cute," said Dawn.

I could feel my eyes getting moist. (I told you, I cry at cat food commercials.) The chimpanzee looked mystified by us.

"This is Angel," Ms. Griswold said in a calm, reassuring voice. "Angel is a very special chimp. She can add and subtract."

She demonstrated by writing $2 + 2 =$ on a blackboard, and passing it into the monkey's cage.

Without letting go of her doll, Angel studied the board for a second and then wrote the number 5 on the board. Then, after thinking for a moment, erased that and wrote 4. We clapped softly.

Dawn leaned over to me and whispered, "Wouldn't it be great if all we had to do to get this kind of approval was add two plus two?"

Then Angel picked up her doll and retreated to a corner of the cage, with her back to us.

"I think Angel is telling us that her performance for today is finished," Ms. Griswold announced. "Wasn't she wonderful?"

Mrs. Gonzalez took over as Ms. Griswold fed Angel a banana. "Angel is with us today because I wanted you to see firsthand just how fascinating an animal can be.

Mrs. Gonzalez nodded to Ms. Harris, who

wheeled in an overhead projector which she aimed at the screen. "I know the everyday study of an animal takes a lot of time. So to make this project easier, I've divided the eighth grade into teams."

"Maybe we'll be on the same one," I said hopefully.

"Not a chance," Dawn murmured. "Whenever teachers put together group projects like this, they deliberately try to keep friends separated. We have two strikes against us already. We're friends *and* stepsisters."

Dawn was right. Moments after Ms. Harris flashed the group lists on the screen, a massive groan rumbled through the auditorium.

Leading the groaning was me. I couldn't believe who was in my group — Howie Johnson and Alan Gray, the most disgusting boys in eighth grade. I threw up my arms in despair. "With those two, no way would we win anything."

"Mine's not so bad," Dawn said cheerily. "In fact, I like my group a lot."

I searched for her name. "Not fair. You're with Logan and Claudia. How did that happen? Want to trade?"

"Not in a million years."

I was so upset about my group arrangement that I wasn't aware of anyone else's predicament.

"Oh, poor Kristy," Dawn said. "What's she going to do?"

From Dawn's reaction, I thought maybe Kristy had ended up with an even more obnoxious person than Alan — if that's possible. "What's the matter?" I asked. "Who's she with?"

"Lauren Hoffman and . . . Stacey."

"But Stacey's a good student," I replied.

"Hello?" Dawn pretended to knock on my head. "Stacey McGill ex-BSC treasurer, remember?"

"Oh, gosh," I said, wide-eyed. "I totally forgot about that."

"The group presenting the best report," continued Mrs. Gonzalez, "will not only receive extra credit on their year-end grade but also a free day's admission to Aqua World in Bridgeport, complete with a personal behind-the-scenes tour."

The auditorium was buzzing with excitement as we headed for our first-period class.

Claudia rushed to Dawn and hugged her. "We're together. All right!"

"Boy, you got to hand it to Gonzalez," Logan said, joining us at the double doors leading out of the auditorium. "She sure knows how to get a project off to a good start."

"You guys, we really have to win," Claudia

said to Dawn and Logan. "I need that extra credit."

"And a visit to Aqua World wouldn't be too bad either, would it?" Logan kidded.

"Attention, students." Alan Gray's voice pierced the air. "You might as well pack it in right now. I have this project, the extra credit, and that trip to Aqua World all sewn up."

"In your dreams, Gray," said Logan. "I'll send you a postcard from Aqua World."

"Don't bother to send it," Alan shot back. "You can hand it to me, because I'll be there before you." The way Alan and Logan talked, you'd think they were the only two students in the competition. Someone needed to explain the meaning of teamwork to them. I hoped it wouldn't have to be me.

That afternoon, I met with my team (Alan and Howie) on the front steps of SMS. It was a short meeting. We didn't discuss the zoo or how much fun the project was going to be. All we talked about was how important it was to win.

"We better get this extra credit or it's — " (Alan drew his finger across his neck making a cutting sound) "for me."

Howie nodded. "Me too."

I got the distinct impression that their grades were in big trouble.

CHAPTER 4

I tried to reassure Alan and Howie that things would be okay.

"I'm going to do my best and work really hard on this project — " I began.

"But I wouldn't count on winning," Logan said, joining us on the steps. He was grinning, but staring straight at Alan.

This was very weird. Logan seemed determined to beat Alan, which of course meant he was determined to beat me.

"Want to make a bet?" Alan challenged him. "How much?"

Logan's jaw tensed for a second, ready to take the challenge. Then he reverted to his friendly, polite self. "I'm sorry, Alan," Logan said with a smile. "But I don't make bets. I think we should just do our project and may the best man — uh, group — win."

A slow smile spread across Alan's face. "Right."

I had been looking forward to the project and spending time at Bedford Zoo, but this rivalry between Logan and Alan added a new, unpleasant twist to things.

That afternoon, during the BSC meeting, I was reminded that I wasn't the only one distressed about the group arrangement.

"I can't ride on the bus with Stacey and spend every afternoon staring at giraffes with her," Kristy moaned to the group. "I mean, that would be totally awful."

"What are you going to do about it?" Claudia asked, passing a bag of pretzels around the room. Everyone took one and chewed intently, thinking about our dilemmas.

"I think we shouldn't go to the zoo," Kristy said with a shrug. "Lauren agrees with me."

"What?" Dawn said. "But that's the fun of the project."

Kristy shook her head. "I can't get on a bus with Stacey and work that closely with her. I'm just not ready to do that."

"But how will you be able to study your animal?" I asked.

"We'll study the everyday habits of dogs," Kristy said. "Separately. Mrs. Gonzalez said we could study our pets. I'll spend my afternoons watching my dog, Shannon. Lauren will study her retriever."

"But Stacey doesn't have a dog," I pointed

out. "She doesn't have a pet of any kind."

"Too bad," Kristy replied stubbornly. "She'll just have to go find one."

Mallory had been quietly listening to all of us complain. "I guess she could study Pow," she said. (Pow is the Pikes' bassett hound.) "He does some amazingly silly things. And since Stacey lives right behind us, it would be easy for her to observe him."

"Good idea, Mal," Kristy said, softening a little. "Maybe Lauren can suggest it to her."

"That solves Kristy's problem," Dawn said, turning to face me. "But what about Mary Anne's?"

I sighed and shook my head. "Mine is more complicated, especially since it involves you and Claudia."

Claudia, who had just shoved a handful of pretzels in her mouth, mumbled, "Pwoblem? Me?"

I explained the Alan Gray versus Logan rivalry that had sprung up that day. "It's weird because, let's face it, we all want to win. But now Alan wants to beat Logan. And Logan really wants to cream Alan. But if Alan gets creamed, so do I."

Claudia listened wide-eyed to what I was saying and then collapsed back against the headboard of her bed. "Whoa."

Then Dawn changed the subject a little. "As

37

long as we're discussing this project, I have to say that I am not a fan of zoos. I feel terrible for the animals, no matter how clean their cages look."

Claudia gulped down the last of her pretzel and turned to Dawn. "You're not suggesting we study house cats like Tigger, are you?"

"Well, uh, no," Dawn stammered. "It's just that . . . well, I just wanted you to know that I'm not crazy about zoos."

"You'll get over it," Claudia said with a wave of her hand. "Especially after you meet Mojo and James."

Dawn squinted one eye shut. "Mojo? The gorilla?"

"That's right," I answered. "I showed you her picture in the paper. Remember?"

"I still think Mojo is a weird name," Dawn remarked, shaking her head. "So who's James?"

Claudia grinned. "Mojo's mate. They're on loan from the San Diego Zoo. And — are you ready for this? Mojo communicates by using American Sign Language."

That excited everyone. Especially Jessi, who was the first of us to learn American Sign Language when she baby-sat for Matt Braddock, who's deaf. The rest of us know enough sign language to sit for Matt, but Jessi's really good at it.

"You could come along as our interpreter," I said to Jessi. "You could ask Mojo questions about her life and what she does in a day."

"Hold it!" Claudia put her hands on her hips. "Jessi will be *our* interpreter. I was the one who mentioned the gorillas first."

My eyes widened. Claudia was sounding as competitive as Logan and Alan. She saw the expression on my face and softened her tone. "I guess Jessi could translate for all of us."

Jessi grinned and made the sign for "okay."

Before we could talk about the project anymore, the phone started ringing. And it rang. And rang. And *rang*. We were swamped.

Dawn took a sitting job with the Gianellis on Tuesday. Shannon accepted one with the Papadakises. I scheduled Kristy and Jessi for Thursday afternoon with the Pike kids, and Mallory took a job with the Hobarts on Friday.

When we finally had a spare second to chat again, the subject turned to the Free Babar campaign.

"I mentioned it to Karen and Andrew and they're really interested," Kristy said.

"You can count the entire Pike family in on this project," Mallory said. "The triplets had a great idea. They suggested we make campaign buttons."

"The kids could design them," Claudia added, inspired. "They could draw elephants on them and maybe put our Babar behind bars."

"Then we could sell them," I suggested. "And donate the proceeds to help find Babar a new home."

Dawn had been quiet during the meeting, except for when she mentioned that she wasn't crazy about zoos. Now she spoke up. "The buttons are a great idea but we need to think bigger in terms of fund-raising. You know, plan something that gets all of Stoneybrook involved."

"Like a bake sale?" I asked.

Dawn shook her head. "Bigger."

"A walkathon," Kristy whispered, staring intently at a spot on Claud's wall. We could practically see the gears turning inside her head. "That would involve everyone. The mayor, the chamber of commerce, the YMCA. We could make the course wind all over Stoneybrook — through downtown and into all the neighborhoods. People who didn't participate in the walk would at least see it pass by their house. We could call it an Elephant Walk."

"Like the song, 'Baby Elephant Walk,' " Jessi said.

Kristy grinned. "Exactly."

As soon as I heard Kristy's good idea, I

kicked into gear. I flipped to the back of the notebook and tried to record what she had just said. "We need to contact the chamber of commerce and the mayor," I murmured as I wrote. "What about the Humane Society?"

Dawn's head bobbed up and down. "I'm sure they'd want to participate. They could pass out fliers and wear those really cute T-shirts they just made up. The ones with the kittens on the front."

"T-shirts!" Claud stood up. "As long as we're making buttons, why don't we make T-shirts, too?"

"Then we could wear them in the Elephant Walk," Mallory said.

"Brilliant!" Kristy cried.

"We'll need to start on this right away," I said. "Tell me what you want to do and I'll write it down. Then we have to call the proper authorities."

"I'll see if Watson will help us on this one," Kristy said. "He knows all of the town's officers."

I nodded as I made a note of it. "And I'll talk to the Free Babar people to find out just what they need."

Claudia turned to Kristy. "I'd like to help you plan a walking course. We can work from a map and design it together."

Mallory raised her hand. "I can write up a special interest story. Maybe the school newspaper will print it."

"I could organize kid groups so they can help brainstorm fund-raising ideas, too," Jessi said. "I'll start with Becca and her friends."

Kristy nodded. "I'll follow up with Karen and her pals."

"And I know seven kids I can talk to," Mallory added with a grin.

"I'll talk to the kids at my school," Shannon offered. "This would be the perfect way to make it a town-wide project. Maybe we can do a carwash or something in addition to the walkathon."

I shook my head in amazement. When the BSC decides to do something, we really go for it. Little Babar would be a free elephant in no time.

CHAPTER 5

"Winners on my side!"

Alan Gray drew an imaginary line with the toe of his tennis shoe across the center aisle of the school bus. "And losers over there." He pointed to the seats behind the bus driver. "Stay put, and you won't have any trouble."

Logan rolled his eyes. "I'm really scared. Come on, Mary Anne," he said, taking my hand and deliberately pulling me across Alan's line. "Let's sit here."

It was Thursday, and we were leaving on our first zoo trip. We were off to an extremely bad start.

Alan and Logan had been making snide comments to each other in the halls, in the lunchroom, and in the yard in front of the school. I thought they were being pretty silly, but I couldn't say anything to either one of them, because I didn't want to be accused of taking sides.

"Are you going to let him sit in that seat?" Howie Johnson whispered to Alan.

"Of course he is," I said. "I'm on your team. And Logan's with me."

Alan thought about that for a few moments, then huffed off to the back row of the school bus. After he sat down, he called to me, "Once we hit the zoo, *he's* not coming with us. No way."

Logan turned around and smiled at Alan. "No problem. I'd much rather spend my time with some *other* animals — like James and Mojo."

Alan turned to Howie and whispered, "Who are they? Some guys from high school?"

Howie laughed so hard he snorted. "James and Mojo are gorillas."

Dawn and Claudia, who were sitting directly across from Logan and me, burst into the giggles, and Alan shot them a dark look. "I knew that."

Mr. Kirkwood, who taught shop, had volunteered to be the driver of our bus. He waited outside until all of the eighth-graders assigned to our bus had boarded. Then he hopped into the driver's seat and pulled the door shut.

"All aboard!" Mr. Kirkwood shouted like a railroad conductor. "Next stop, Bedford Zoo!"

We pulled out of the school parking lot, and followed the tree-lined streets to the edge of town. As we turned onto the highway, several spitballs zinged over our heads. I didn't have to turn around. I could guess where they'd come from.

"Oh, gross!" Shawna Riverson cried from two seats in front of me. "Alan and Howie are shooting spitballs."

Hannah Toce looked over her shoulder and snapped, "Why don't you two grow up?"

Then Claudia and Dawn both turned around and said, "Yeah. Grow up!"

Howie and Alan crossed their eyes and made faces at the front of the bus.

"Jerks," Hannah said as a general announcement to the rest of the bus. A low murmur and bobbing of heads signaled that everyone agreed with her.

Logan squeezed my hand. "Poor Mary Anne," he murmured. "Stuck with those guys for three weeks."

I wanted to tell Logan that he could help make things a lot easier if he'd stop bumping heads with Alan, but I lost my nerve. I was afraid Logan might think I was siding with Alan.

The rest of the ride was without incident, thank goodness. For a moment it looked as if we were actually going to have a pretty calm afternoon. But as the bus pulled into the parking lot, we were met by a small crowd of about ten people, waving signs in front of the bus.

"Zoos are cruel. Don't go in there!" one gray-haired woman cried.

"Whoa," Logan said. "It looks like the animal rights people don't like Bedford Zoo."

I was worried. "Do you think we'll have to fight our way through the picket line?"

"Hardly," Logan said, chuckling. "I think this is as active as these protesters get. Don't worry, they can't stop us from entering the zoo."

"They can't stop us," Claudia agreed, watching the group intently from her side of the bus, "but they can certainly make us feel bad."

"Kids, listen up," Mr. Kirkwood called from the front of the bus. "When you get off the bus, don't dawdle. Go straight into the visitors' center." He looked at us in the rearview mirror, his mouth drawn tight. "Is that clear?"

We nodded silently.

He pulled forward, leaving the protesters behind, and drove to the front gate of the zoo. He stopped the bus and we filed out so fast, I think we set a field trip record. No one wanted to talk to the picketers.

Once the last student was inside the visitors' center, everyone relaxed. The walls were covered with large, colorful photos of Bengal tigers, giraffes, polar bears, flamingos, elephants, and camels. Purple-and-green nylon banners hung from the ceiling. On each banner was the profile of an animal. At one end of the room, cedar benches had been arranged in rows facing a small platform. The space was light and airy and made you feel good. I hoped the rest of the zoo made you feel the same way.

"Good afternoon," said a pleasant woman with blonde hair in a blunt, chin-length cut as she took her place on the platform. She was tanned and slender and wore a navy blue skirt and blazer. "I'm Mrs. Wofsey, the director of Bedford Zoo. As soon as you take your seats, we'll begin our presentation."

Alan and Howie grabbed the bench right in front of Mrs. Wofsey. I decided I had better join them so I said good-bye to Logan and slid onto the bench beside Howie. Alan leaned over and whispered, "Glad to see you're back on the winning team."

All of this talk of winning was getting pretty tedious but I smiled anyway. (That's me — Miss Don't-Make-Waves.)

"Now the first thing I'd like to do is introduce my assistant, Mr. Chester." Mrs. Wofsey gestured to a short, heavy-set man in a blue blazer standing in the corner. He was bald and wore gold-rimmed glasses. He didn't smile or say hi, but just gave us a brisk nod.

"I'll bet he's a lot of fun at parties," Howie cracked. I gave him a nudge with my elbow to silence him.

"Mr. Chester and I are very proud of our zoo," Mrs. Wofsey continued. "And we're excited about some of our recent acquisitions."

The lights dimmed and a picture flashed on the wall behind her. It looked like a small television painted bright red. On the side was a keyhole.

"This is one of our new key-activated information boxes. Visitors to the zoo pay a one-dollar fee and receive a key, like this." Mrs. Wofsey held up a gold key. "This allows them to unlock our information boxes, and browse through the material. Don't worry, it's basic background information and won't interfere with your research."

Mrs. Wofsey pulled another key out of her pocket. It looked identical to the first one. "This is my zoo key. You'll notice that the info keys are replicas of the keys the zoo employees use to enter the animal cages."

"Whoa," Alan murmured, leaning forward intensely. "You don't think — ?"

Mrs. Wofsey cut him off with a steely look. "Now don't get the idea that your keys will unlock the cages, because they won't. The keys only *look* identical."

Alan actually blushed. I knew Logan, sitting

behind us, was thoroughly enjoying Alan's humiliation.

"Mr. Chester is going to give each one of you your own key," Mrs. Wofsey continued, "so that you can have access to the same information as any regular zoo visitor. I only ask that you take good care of them and at the end of three weeks, please return them."

I'll have to admit, having my own key to the zoo was pretty exciting. Mr. Chester walked down the rows of benches and passed out the keys. When he was finished he turned to face Mrs. Wofsey. He looked as if he were expecting her to give him another set of orders.

Mrs. Wofsey smiled at her assistant. "Mr. Chester, why don't you tell the group about our most exciting project?"

Strangely, Mr. Chester didn't seem to share Mrs. Wofsey's enthusiasm about anything. He just shrugged and started talking to us, saying in a flat voice, "The zoo has received a pair of gorillas on loan from San Diego. We'll have them for four weeks."

"Their names are Mojo and James," Mrs. Wofsey jumped in. "And they're delightful. Mojo has been taught American Sign Language, and can actually communicate with her trainers — when she's in the right mood. We're extremely pleased to have them with us. There is one problem, however." Mrs. Wofsey paused to clasp her hands in front of her, then took a deep breath. "Shortly before Mojo and James arrived, we began to receive disturbing notes saying things like, 'Cages are cruel,' and, 'Animals should be free.' There were enough of them to make us worry that some disgruntled person might try to let the animals out of their cages. Mojo and James are our guests and it's of the utmost importance that we protect them, as well as all of the other animals here at Bedford Zoo. For that reason, I've hired extra security guards to patrol the zoo. They'll be on duty around the clock."

Mrs. Wofsey hadn't specifically mentioned the people with the picket signs but I was sure that's who she meant the animals needed to be protected from. I'd read about animal rights activists who set laboratory animals free, so I wouldn't have been surprised if one of them did try to let the animals out of their cages.

Then Mr. Chester stepped forward and gave us a quick rundown of the zoo regulations. They were pretty standard. Don't litter. Don't feed the animals. Never stick your hand in a cage. Try to be respectful and not scare the animals in any way. Even Howie and Alan found it easy to agree to follow those rules.

"All right then." Mrs. Wofsey clapped her

hands together. "You have an hour and a half. Enjoy yourselves."

Howie, Alan, and I decided that we would circle the zoo and each make a list of the top three animals we would like to study.

"Then we'll compare notes," I said, "and make our selection."

I watched to see which way Logan, Claudia, and Dawn went, and then deliberately headed our group in the opposite direction.

Here's the most bizarre thing about the afternoon — Howie, Alan, and I actually enjoyed ourselves. The sun was shining, and the animals seemed to have spring fever. They all looked interesting. It was going to be hard to choose just one to study. On the bus ride back to school, everyone talked nonstop about the animals. Logan and Alan didn't say one mean thing to each other.

CHAPTER 6

Thursday

Beware of the words, "Some Assembly Required." They mean, "It will take you hours and you will go crazy."

Kristy is talking about the button-making machine Nicky got from my grandparents. We've never been able to make it work. Until today.

Mal and I slaved over the machine for practically the whole sitting job. Then when we finally did figure it out, I kind of wished we hadn't...

The Free Babar project was now in full swing. We'd talked to all of our regular clients, and the kids were anxious to do whatever they could to save that little elephant.

The Pike kids were particularly interested. Since their suggestion of making Free Babar buttons had been taken up by the BSC, they'd hardly talked about anything else. None of Mallory's seven brothers and sisters thought of Thursday as a baby-sitting day. It was E (for elephant)-Day.

Mallory met Kristy at the door that afternoon. "Come on in. The kids have been waiting for you. We've turned the kitchen into the art room. And the dining room is the button shop."

"Button shop?" Kristy peered around the door of the dining room. Nicky and the triplets, Byron, Jordan, and Adam, were all wearing visors of varying types and sitting around the dining room table. In the center of the table sat something that looked like a weird stapler.

"What is that?" Kristy asked. "It looks dangerous."

"It's my button-maker," Nicky said, smiling proudly. "Grandma and Grandpa gave it to me, but we can't figure out how it works."

"Are there instructions?" Kristy asked, joining the boys at the table.

Jordan held up a crumpled piece of paper. "Yes. But no one can understand them."

"We've each taken a turn at it," Mallory explained, "but so far we've struck out. We're hoping you can do it."

Kristy examined the instructions, muttering to herself and pointing to the different parts of the stamp machine as she read. After a few minutes she looked up. "It says we're supposed to have perfectly cut round circles of paper that will go over the metal backs."

Mal nodded. "We've got those. Margo, Vanessa, and Claire are working on the drawings in the kitchen — excuse me, the art room."

"Let's go see."

The kitchen table was covered with Magic Markers, glitter pens, glue, and pictures of elephants. Some Babar books lay open for reference.

"Awfully quiet in here," Kristy murmured to Mallory as they watched the girls work.

Mal nodded. "They take this button business very seriously. Their pictures of Babar have to be perfect. At least that's what Margo told me."

Margo looked up. "I decided just to do Babar's head. Does it look okay?"

Claire peered over Margo's shoulder. "It looks like a dog with big ears."

Margo was crestfallen. "It does?"

"Of course not," said Kristy. "If you make the nose just a little bit longer, it will be perfect. Also, put a bit of Babar's green suit in the picture and everyone will know who he is right away."

"Especially if we write Free Babar on the buttons," Vanessa pointed out.

"Vanessa hasn't drawn one elephant picture," Margo complained. "I've had to do them all."

Vanessa was bent over her paper, working diligently. Scattered on the floor around her were crumpled pieces of paper.

"If you're not painting Babar," Kristy asked, "what are you doing?"

"I've written a poem," Vanessa said, blushing slightly. She kept her arm crooked around her paper. "But it's not ready yet so don't anybody look."

Mallory patted her on the shoulder. "Come on, Vanessa, let's hear it. It doesn't have to be finished."

Vanessa thought about it for a second, then moved her arm. "You read it," she said to Mal.

> *"Babar the elephant*
> *Is very, very sad.*
> *If you help him find a home*
> *He will be oh, so glad."*

"That's really great, Vanessa," Kristy said. "Don't change a word."

"Now we have two kinds of buttons to sell," Kristy said.

"Three!" Claire held up her drawing. It was an elephant with a banana almost his size next to him.

"Three!" Kristy took Claire's button drawing. "Good work, guys."

Mallory raised one finger. "We don't exactly have the buttons yet. Remember, we can't make the machine work."

Kristy rubbed her hands together. "I read the instructions. We'll be making buttons in no time."

"Here." Margo handed her the picture of the dog with big ears. "Do this one first. I made a bigger nose and wrote 'Free Babar' on it."

"Write 'Free Babar' on mine, too," Claire cried.

"I'll do it," Mallory said, taking the drawing and printing the words in her best calligraphy.

"Here we go!" Kristy took the first buttons to the dining room to assemble them in the machine.

Mallory stayed with the girls, helping Margo draw elephant noses that were big enough, and gathering Claire's banana drawings. She was also ready to help Vanessa with her spell-

56

ing, which tended to be creative.

Meanwhile in the dining room, Kristy tinkered with the Badge-o-matic, reading the instructions out loud as she followed them. "First, place the big ring in your palm and set the metal back, the artwork, and the plastic cover in its center. Be sure they're dead center. Now put the thin ring on top of that, and the lid over that. Put your other hand over your palm and press the pieces together. But not too hard."

"This is confusing," Nicky said.

"You're telling me," Kristy muttered. She looked at the paper again. "Now place the metal backing on top, flip it over, and place the entire button in the Badge-o-matic. Press down lever."

Adam pushed down the lever. *"Voilà!"*

Nicky held up a perfectly shaped button with Claire's elephant in the middle. "Look! Our first button!"

"All right!" The triplets gave each other and Kristy high-fives.

Kristy studied the instructions again. "It looks like the problem spot happens when you put the metal clasp on the back, press down with your palm, and flip the badge. That's probably where things go wrong."

"No. We got confused way before that," Nicky said.

"Well, we know what we're doing now," Kristy replied. "We can declare the Badge-o-matic factory officially open."

Margo's picture was done next, and then came Vanessa's poem. In the meantime, Claire had made several more elephants and Mallory had joined in with her own interpretation of Babar. By the end of an hour they had successfully assembled twelve buttons.

"I think we should start selling them," Vanessa said.

"But don't you want to make more?" Kristy asked.

"No!" Claire shook her head furiously. "We need money for Babar. Right now."

Kristy looked at Mallory and shrugged. "I guess we can do a test run. You know, just to see if anyone is interested in buying them."

Mal checked her watch. "We have one more hour before Mom and Dad are due home. That'll give us enough time to cover a good chunk of the neighborhood."

Kristy nodded. "Why don't we divide into two groups? You take your kids to the neighbors around your house, making sure to hit Burnt Hill Road and Elm Street. And I'll take my group over to Bradford Court, Fawcett Avenue, and Kimball Street."

Vanessa found two baskets, and the kids carefully divided up the buttons, six in each.

Then Byron, Margo, and Claire went off with Kristy, while Mallory took Vanessa and the rest of the boys with her.

"Hold it!" Kristy shouted when Mallory and the others were halfway across the lawn. "We haven't settled on a price for the buttons."

"One million dollars!" Claire cried.

Mallory looked down at the basket. "A dollar?"

"No." Byron crossed his arms stubbornly. "They're worth more than that."

Mallory shrugged. "Five dollars?"

As usual, Kristy was the one with the best idea. "I know. We'll say, 'These are on sale for a suggested donation of five dollars. If you can't afford that, we'll take less. If you'd like to give more, that would be wonderful, too.' "

"Excellent!" Adam cried, pumping his fist in the air. "They'll probably give us ten!"

The kids raced out of the yard with their baskets, looking like Halloween trick-or-treaters heading for their first house. Kristy and Mal made sure they guided their charges toward a few surefire wins.

Mallory and her group stopped at the Braddocks' house first. Haley answered the door. She already knew about the Free Babar campaign and hurried to find her mom.

When Mrs. Braddock appeared, Matt was also by her side. She signed to him that we were selling the buttons and that he could pick one. He pointed to Margo's and chuckled, signing something too quickly for Mal to understand. His mother translated. "Matt says he wants to buy that one because it looks like a dog with big ears."

Mal was glad Margo wasn't in her group. She knew her sister would have been mortified.

The kids knew how to sign, "See you later." They shouted good-bye to Haley, who called back, "Next time you make buttons, let me know. I draw great elephants."

While Mallory's group headed for the Prezziosos' house, Kristy led her group to Bradford Court. Mrs. Newton was happy to buy a badge.

"Look!" Vanessa pointed at the money they received. "She gave us a ten-dollar bill."

Adam and Nicky gave each other high-fives. "Score!"

Then while Mallory's group hit the Perkinses' house, Kristy's went to the Marshalls' and the Mancusis'.

"This is amazing," Margo cried as she skipped down the street. "Everyone is giving more than five dollars. With all this money, Babar will be free in no time."

Kristy checked her watch. "We have time

for one more house and then we need to head back home."

"The Johanssens!" Nicky raced up the walk and pushed the doorbell. Kristy and the others hurried behind him, the kids calling, "Wait for us, Nicky. We have the buttons."

Nicky put his ear against the door. "They're home. I can hear footsteps and voices."

The kids, their best sales-pitch smiles plastered on their faces, struck a group pose in front of the door. Kristy stood behind them, her face frozen in a smile, too.

That smile disappeared the moment the door opened. Charlotte was standing in the Johanssens' foyer. And behind her, much to Kristy's surprise, was her baby-sitter.

"Stacey!" Kristy gasped. "What are you doing here?"

"Baby-sitting," Stacey replied. "What does it look like?"

"But — but you're not part of the club anymore," Kristy spluttered. "How can you baby-sit?"

"Dr. Johanssen *asked* me to sit, that's how." Stacey stared Kristy in the eye.

"But the Johanssens are *our* clients," Kristy continued.

Stacey shrugged. "I guess they realized what a special relationship Char and I have, so they called me first."

61

There was a lot Kristy wanted to say to Stacey, but she didn't, mostly because the kids were right there. Instead she said, "Well, I guess we can't prevent you from taking jobs — "

"I guess you can't," Stacey cut in. "Besides, I thought this would be a good opportunity for me to work on our biology project. I've decided to observe Carrot."

Carrot is Charlotte's schnauzer. At the mention of his name, he came racing to the door, barking.

"See?" Stacey gestured toward Carrot. "I guess I'll write down that he barks when strange people come to the door."

That did it. If Kristy wasn't seeing red before, she was now. She told me later that if she'd been a cartoon character, steam would have shot out of her ears.

There was an uncomfortable silence as Kristy and Stacey glared at each other, fighting back what they really wanted to say. Finally Charlotte broke the tension.

"What's in the basket?" she asked, stepping out onto the porch.

"A Free Babar button," Nicky replied. "Want to buy one?"

"Sorry, Nicky," Stacey said, in a much warmer voice than she'd used with Kristy. "Neither Charlotte nor I have any money.

Why don't you come back later when the Johanssens are home?"

"Fine with me." Kristy was already off the porch and walking down the sidewalk. "Come on, kids. Time to head back."

" 'Bye, Charlotte!" the kids shouted. " 'Bye!"

"See you later," Charlotte called back.

Neither Stacey nor Kristy said good-bye to each other. They were both too mad.

CHAPTER 7

"Everyone wants to study either the gorillas or the monkeys," I pointed out to Alan on Friday. We had just arrived at the zoo and were standing near the primate enclosure. "We should pick animals that are different."

Alan narrowed his eyes at me suspiciously. "Is Logan's group studying the gorillas?"

"Yes," I admitted. "But that's not why I want to observe a different animal. It's because I talked to Hannah Toce and Emily Bernstein and both of their groups will be watching Mojo and James, too."

Alan nudged Howie. "I think Mary Anne wants to let her boyfriend win."

"I do not," I said huffily. "*I* want to win. That extra credit would mean as much to me as it would to Logan. Maybe more."

Science is not one of my strong points, even though I really like it. Logan, on the other hand, is a natural at it. He rarely studies for tests.

"I think it would be good to do something really different, like choosing three different types of animals — one from the water, one that flies, and one that lives on land — and calling our report *Fur, Feathers, and Fins.*"

"I want to study Mojo and James," Howie said, stubbornly folding his arms across his chest. His face, which is covered in freckles, grew redder and redder as we talked.

The three of us were still arguing when Logan, Dawn, and Claudia arrived. They'd been at the front gate gathering brochures about the special exhibits at the zoo.

"I see you all are getting along quite nicely." Logan smirked as he, Claudia, and Dawn passed by.

"This is a private meeting," Alan shot back. "Do you mind?"

"Well, ex-*cuuuuuuse* me," Logan replied. Then he turned to Dawn and Claudia and drawled, "That's my idea of a fun meeting — yell at each other and turn red in the face."

Logan's remarks were starting to get on my nerves. I turned to Alan and said in a voice that I hoped Logan would overhear, "Ignore him, Alan. We have to do things our own way."

Alan took a couple of deep breaths and then turned to Howie. "I agree with Mary Anne about Mojo and James. I mean, look, all the kids are watching the gorillas. And I think the fur, feathers, and fins idea is great — with one change."

"What's that?" I asked, pleased that things were going more smoothly.

"Instead of fins, why don't we call it flippers?" Alan suggested. "That way we can study the seals. They're a lot of fun to watch."

"Fine with me." I took my spiral notebook out of my backpack and wrote the words *Fur, Feathers, and Flippers* at the top of the page. It was now official.

Howie didn't look very pleased about the new turn of events, but all he said was, "I get to pick the fur animal."

"Okay," I said. "Which one do you want? Tigers?"

Howie shook his head. "Bears."

Alan and I thought bears would be fine. That left me the feathers category. I turned slowly in a circle, looking at the cages for inspiration. The animals from Australia were near the primate enclosure. "I choose the emu," I said.

"Fine," Alan said.

"Whatever that is," Howie grumbled in reply.

Then we split up, each one of us going off to observe the animal we'd selected.

I strolled over to the Australian animal pen, which was basically a small pasture with some trees and a few covered barns. A big gate near the primates ran across a cement drive used by zoo maintenance and veterinary trucks to drive in and out of the penned area.

I found an empty bench and started observing the emu. For your information, an emu basically looks a lot like an ostrich but has big gray feathers. I wrote down everything I could see, then used my zoo key in the information box to find out more:

The emu, at six feet tall, is second in height only to the ostrich. A friendly and curious bird, the emu wanders the arid plains of Australia. (I found this next part interesting.) *The female lays the eggs but it is the sole responsibility of the male to incubate and raise the young. They eat a diet consisting primarily of grasses, fruits, seeds, and berries and can live to be over forty years old.*

Once I'd written down the information about the emu, I watched. And watched. And watched. I hate to admit it but a half an hour of emu-watching was about all I could stand. All the emu did was sit underneath a scraggly shade tree, looking like a great big chicken. One time it did cross the enclosure to get a drink of water from a large wooden trough, but it returned immediately to its spot under that tree. I decided to wander around the zoo and come back later.

Before I left, I watched some kangaroos, which were really cute. A group of SMS students had gathered to watch a mother kangaroo, whose baby was hanging out of her pouch. "Look, there's the baby joey," said one.

"I think I'll call them Kanga and Roo," Erica Blumberg replied, making a note in her book. "After the mother and baby in the Winnie-the-Pooh books."

I started to say, "We're supposed to observe the animals, not name them," but I stopped myself. If it makes observing them for hours on end easier, I thought to myself, then let her name the animals anything she wants.

I continued on my walk, wondering what name I should give my emu. Emily? Elizabeth? Edith?

"Edith the emu," I said out loud.

"Talking to yourself already?" a familiar voice said behind me.

I spun around, giggling. "Dawn, you caught me. I've just spent thirty minutes watching an emu sit and blink its eyes. That can make you a little loony."

"We've been observing Mojo and James," Dawn said. "It's really eerie. Like being a peeping tom at someone's window."

Suddenly, loud shouts came from near the entrance to the zoo.

"Stop the cruelty! Free our animals!"

Dawn and I watched as the protesters, who must have paid the entry fee to get onto the grounds, marched toward the primate area.

"Please, help stop the cruelty." A young woman with long brown hair, wearing a floral print skirt, and pink T-shirt, pressed a brochure into Dawn's hand. "Mojo and James should be allowed to roam free."

Dawn studied the brochure. "It does seem cruel to keep animals in these cages. I mean, Mojo's and James's cage is certainly bigger than a little wire cage, but it says here that gorillas like Mojo and James are used to roaming two or three miles in a day. This must be like torture to them."

I love animals, and I always worry when I visit a zoo that the animals aren't being treated well, but Mrs. Wofsey seemed to be a kind, caring person. And the Bedford Zoo had a really nice feel to it.

"I don't know. These animals seem happy," I said to Dawn. "The cages are clean and they're fed regularly. And I think Bedford Zoo has done a pretty good job recreating the animals' natural habitats."

"But things could get too crowded," Dawn

said. "I mean, look how many of the animals have had babies. That practically doubles the number that have to share those spaces."

I didn't want to argue with Dawn. I'd had my share of arguing for the day. So I was relieved when Claudia caught up with us and said her aunt was here and it was time to go.

Claud, Dawn, and I had planned to cut short our Friday zoo visit. We planned to return on Saturday. Mrs. Wofsey had given us a sneak preview of the weekend's events, and they sounded like a lot of fun.

Our Friday BSC meeting was a zoo itself. The biology project made scheduling a nightmare. Dawn, Claudia, and I had several afternoons reserved for animal watching at the zoo.

Luckily, Dawn came up with the brilliant idea of mixing work with work. When the Arnolds called looking for a sitter for Marilyn and Carolyn on Saturday afternoon, Dawn asked if it would be all right to take the girls to the zoo. The Arnolds were delighted.

The next day Claudia's mom dropped me, Logan, and Claudia off at the zoo. Alan and Howie were waiting for me by the front gate.

"Don't start anything, please," I murmured to Logan, who shot me a "Who, me?" wounded look.

Howie and Alan said hi to Claudia and me,

and completely ignored Logan. I was relieved. Silence was better than all that bickering.

"I'm going to run on ahead," Logan said. I could tell he was a little hurt by my remark. "I'll catch up with you later."

He wove his way through the small group of protesters outside the entrance. By now they seemed as much a part of the zoo as the ticket takers. They were marching up and down the walk, chanting, "No more cages! No more cages!"

For a second I thought about the letters Mrs. Wofsey had talked about. Would these people really follow through with their threats? I hoped not.

As we passed through the turnstiles, I could see Dawn and the Arnold twins heading our way.

"Hi, Mary Anne! Hi, Claudia!" Marilyn and Carolyn ran toward us. They were eager to tell us their news. Marilyn had lost a tooth, and a new one was starting to grow in Carolyn's mouth. Marilyn was gearing up for another piano recital.

"We're just in time for the elephant art exhibition," Claudia announced.

Although Alan and Howie were keeping their distance, they were close enough to hear what Claudia said. "What's that?" Alan asked with a scowl.

"Oh, I read about that," I said. "The elephants are given big housepainting brushes and a huge easel and they paint with their trunks. It should be really fun to watch."

Howie nudged Alan with his elbow. "Not my idea of fun."

"Not mine either," said Marilyn.

Dawn draped her arm over Marilyn's shoulder and explained to us, "We just went to see the tigers. They were all inside and it upset Marilyn to see them in such small cages."

"They just paced back and forth, back and forth," Marilyn said, rocking right and left as she spoke. "It's so sad."

"Well, the art exhibit won't be sad," I said. "You'll get to see the elephants having fun."

Alan tapped me on the shoulder. "I don't feel like watching a bunch of elephants paint. I think I'll go do some more seal watching. Two o'clock is their feeding time."

"Yeah, I don't feel like watching Jumbo paint, either," Howie chimed in. "I think I'll check up on the bears. See how they're doing. Yesterday, they just slept. Maybe they'll be awake today."

"Okay." I checked my watch. "We better hurry, the exhibition starts in two minutes."

A small crowd had already assembled in the amphitheater outside the elephant house. The amphitheater consisted of several rows of wooden benches set in half circles up the side of a small hill, looking down on the elephants' play yard. The yard was empty except for a row of large easels set with blank sheets of cardboard, a table with several paintbrushes on it, and a large garbage can. Mrs. Wofsey was just finishing some announcements to the audience when we arrived.

"Please take your seats, everyone," she said. "The elephants will be out in just a few minutes."

"I want to sit in front," Carolyn said.

"I want to sit with you," Marilyn said, taking Dawn's hand.

The benches were filling up fast, especially the ones in front so Dawn said quickly, "All right, Carolyn, you sit in the front row, but when it's over, wait for me to come find you. I'll be in back."

We hurried up the hillside and slipped onto a bench near the back. Music blared from loudspeakers set into the foliage at the front of the amphitheater, and the elephants' barn doors were thrown open.

"Look!" cried Marilyn, as two adult elephants and a smaller, younger one marched in a perfect line into the play yard. "They're wearing big hats."

"Those are called berets," Dawn explained. "A lot of artists wear them."

"The elephants are so cute," I cried. "Especially the little one. Oooh, look at him!"

The smaller elephant, who had been trotting behind the grown-up ones, suddenly sprinted ahead of the others to grab his paintbrush. Then he raced to the large garbage can, which was full of paint, and dipped his brush in it. He trotted around in a half circle leaving a big red stripe on every easel.

"You little rascal," the elephant handler scolded. "Now come on. Up to your easel. Up!"

The two larger elephants took their artwork more seriously. They were already painting around the red stripes on their canvases. It was fascinating watching them choose among the primary colors of red, yellow, and blue. Sometimes they'd mix them and get a bright green or reddish-purple.

Our seats were close to the side of the amphitheater, where Mrs. Wofsey was standing and watching the show. So we were the first to hear the bad news when Mr. Chester delivered it to her.

"The emu. She escaped," Mr. Chester said, puffing, red in the face.

"Oh, my word." Mrs. Wofsey reached for the walkie-talkie in a belt on her hip and started barking orders. "I'll call zoo security.

You get Mike and Curtis from the plant crew, and we'll cordon off the area."

"No need," Mr. Chester said, finally catching his breath. "I've already taken care of the problem. The vet was in the area. He drove the zoo cart while I herded the emu back into her pen."

Mrs. Wofsey put her walkie-talkie back in its holster. "Well, I'm glad you've handled it so efficiently. Fortunately, the emu is a fairly tame bird. I'm glad Tim was there to help you. Thank you."

Mr. Chester smiled. "It was nothing."

"I think I'd better get over there to see how the escape occurred," Mrs. Wofsey said.

"Don't worry, that's under control as well," Mr. Chester said. "I'm having some of the groundskeepers look into it."

"I'm sorry, but that won't do." Mrs. Wofsey's voice was stern. "As head of this zoo, it's my job to make sure these things don't happen. I will conduct this investigation personally."

Mr. Chester shrugged. "Suit yourself."

This new information was far more intriguing than the painting demonstration. Especially since it involved *my* emu, Edith. It was hard to imagine her staging a break-out.

When the elephant exhibition ended, I said

a quick good-bye to Dawn and hurried to the emu's pen to see what had happened. I figured this would be something exciting to write in my journal.

Friday: Edith slept, took two drinks of water.

Saturday: Edith slept, took one drink of water, then broke down the fence and escaped.

I think my imagination went a little wild. When I reached the pen, I could see that the fence was just fine. In fact, there was no sign of any disturbance at all. As usual, Edith was under her tree, dozing.

Mrs. Wofsey was inside, on the concrete driveway, talking to a man sitting behind the wheel of what looked like a golf cart. The words *Bedford Zoo — Veterinary Services* were painted on the side. I figured that the man was Tim, who had helped Mr. Chester corral Edith.

Several other students and visitors had gathered by the gate to see what the commotion was about. Upon seeing the crowd, Mrs. Wofsey walked over to the fence to make an announcement.

"Some of you may have heard that our emu escaped from her pen about an hour ago. This is true. But as you can see she is back, safe and sound. You have nothing to be concerned about. As you know, if you have used your gold key and listened to the info kiosk, the emu is a very docile bird. No one was in any danger of getting hurt."

While Mrs. Wofsey was talking, I noticed several large red stains on the concrete at her feet. Not bloodstains, but more like the stains left by smashed berries. They were just inside the gate, and also on my side (the public side) of the drive. I wondered if someone had spilled a bucket full of berries.

The crowd stayed for a few more minutes. Maybe they wanted to see if Edith would make another break for it. But as she settled in for what was probably going to be a long afternoon nap, they wandered off. I watched Mrs. Wofsey and Tim talk for a while. At one point she turned in a half circle, gesturing at the fence ringing the perimeter of the field. I guessed she was asking Tim to check it for any breaks.

As he drove away, she reached in the pocket of her jacket, then spun around, looking at the ground.

"Curtis!" she called to a man in a green shirt and green work pants. He held a broom and dust pan in his hand and was busily picking up litter and dumping it in the trash. Curtis hurried over to the gate.

"Yes, Mrs. Wofsey?"

"Have you seen my master key? I seem to have misplaced it." Mrs. Wofsey sounded anxious. "You know what it looks like, don't you? It's brass, like those gold-painted keys the visitors use for the kiosks."

"I'll keep an eye out for it," Curtis replied.

"Thank you." Mrs. Wofsey checked her pockets once more, shaking her head nervously.

Out of the corner of my eye, I caught some movement a few yards away, near the primate enclosure. It was Mr. Chester. I think he had overheard Mrs. Wofsey's conversation. He was making a clucking sound of disapproval with his tongue.

I had just decided to help Mrs. Wofsey look for her key when I felt a tap on my shoulder. "Yikes!" I squealed.

"Boy, are you jumpy," Alan said.

I told them about the emu's escape, recapping Mr. Chester's tale of herding the emu back to its pen. They were pretty impressed.

"I wish the seals had been that exciting," Alan said. "Two o'clock was feeding time, I thought. But by the time I got there, they were taking their afternoon nap. The attendant said they'd already eaten."

I jotted his observation in my notebook: "Seals nap soon after eating." Then I turned to Howie. "How'd it go with the bears?"

"The bears?" Howie blinked at me for a second. "Oh, right. The bears. Um, they mostly lounged around on tree branches, napping."

"All afternoon?" I asked.

"Pretty much." Howie grinned crookedly. "Nice life those bears have. Eat and then loaf around in your big fur coat."

"Boring," Alan said.

I checked the notebook entries. There was a full page on the emu, and only one measly sentence each on the seals and bears. "Wasn't there anything else you observed about your animals?" I asked them.

Howie scratched his head. "I didn't notice anything else about the bears but I did see something strange outside the bear cage. This couple wearing matching sweatsuits and lugging a lot of camera equipment were walking around. They'd stop at a cage and talk a lot, then make notes on a pad. But here's the weird part — they never took any pictures."

"I'm sure they were just visiting the zoo," I said. "I mean, lots of people carry cameras."

Howie shook his head. "These guys didn't seem like normal tourist types. I mean, they weren't enjoying looking at the animals. I didn't see them smile once. But they sure talked a lot about each animal."

My dad picked up Claudia, Logan, and me and drove us home. On the way back, the image of Edith sitting docilely under her tree kept popping into my head. It wasn't until we were pulling into the driveway that the thought finally hit me. Edith didn't escape . . . somebody must have let her out. But who? The protestors in front of the zoo? And what about the strange couple in the matching sweatsuits? Hmm. It looked like we had a mystery on our hands. One that needed to be solved soon.

CHAPTER 8

"The emu couldn't have escaped, because all she does is eat and sit. I would have to say that bird is the least likely candidate for a breakout at Bedford Zoo," I said at the Monday BSC meeting. "Add the fact that there was no break in the fence and I think we have a mystery on our hands."

We discussed the threatening notes Mrs. Wofsey had received, the protestors who marched in front of the zoo, and the weird couple with the camera equipment.

"I think I saw those two," Dawn said. "I don't remember what they looked like but I do remember their matching sweatsuits."

Claudia, who was on her hands and knees looking for a shoebox in her closet, called, "Watch out for matching sweatsuits. I hate it when couples dress alike. It's so geeky."

"I noticed something else odd," I said,

"which may or may not have anything to do with the mystery of who freed Edith."

"Edith?" Kristy cut in. "Who's Edith?"

I could feel myself blush. "The emu. I named her that because I was tired of staring at her and just thinking of her as *the emu*."

"Oh, okay." Kristy flicked her wrist in the air. "Go on."

"Well, I noticed some huge red berry stains on the drive, just inside the gate and on the public side of the drive. I know they weren't there on Friday because I spent Friday afternoon watching her and staring at her pen."

"This is a mystery," Kristy murmured.

"One that the BSC could probably solve," I said. "Most of us are there every day — "

"And since we love animals," Dawn cut in, "we could be doing something to help them."

"While you are observing the animals be sure to keep a close watch on people," Kristy directed. "Make a note of anyone doing anything suspicious. Keep track of the time that you saw them as well as the location."

"We should also make a note of the location of any bushes with red berries," I said.

"Ah! Here it is!" Claudia exclaimed suddenly. She held up an open shoebox with a bag of Oreos tucked inside. "Cookies, anyone?"

We passed the shoebox around the circle, each of us taking a cookie.

Kristy took a bite of hers and mused, "I wish my group was going to the zoo. I spent the weekend watching Shannon. I had no idea she did so little with her day. Basically, she drinks a lot of water, with huge strings of slobber hanging from her mouth — "

"Ew!" we all cried, wrinkling our noses. "Gross!"

Kristy ignored us. "Then she wanders from room to room looking for playmates. Then she flops down in the middle of doorsills where people have to step over her. The high point of her day is barking at the mailman."

"It's not too late to change your project," I said. "You could join us at the zoo."

"I can't," Kristy said, taking another cookie. "Because of Stacey and Lauren, remember?"

"Maybe Lauren and Stacey want to change, too," Claudia suggested.

"That would mean talking to Stacey," Kristy said. "And then, if she didn't want to change, I'd have to argue with her. No thanks."

Mallory, whose backyard backs up to Stacey's backyard, asked, "How long do you think we can go on not speaking like this?"

Kristy pursed her lips. "Until she decides to apologize."

"Which will be never," Claudia said. "I don't think Stacey feels that she owes anyone an apology."

Kristy shrugged. "Then we could go on forever."

That was a depressing thought. So depressing that for a full minute no one spoke. We just sat with our shoulders slumped, thinking about not ever speaking to Stacey again.

Luckily, the phone rang and we had to concentrate on work. Jessi took a job sitting for the Braddocks and then Shannon scheduled a job watching the Gianellis.

I had wanted to talk more about the mystery and discuss my Logan vs. Alan problem, but I never had a chance. The rest of the half hour was completely taken up booking jobs.

On Tuesday afternoon at the zoo I noticed some new people on the staff. All of them carried walkie-talkies and wore navy blue blazers with the bright yellow *Bedford Zoo* patch on the breast pocket.

"Security has been tightened," Alan commented, as Howie and I joined him at a picnic table in the snack area. "I've counted at least four new employees."

So the zoo officials thought somebody had let Edith out, too. That made me more determined to find out who had done it.

Meanwhile, Howie was digging around in his pocket. "I can't believe it," he muttered. "I just can't believe it."

"You can't believe what?" Alan and I asked at the same time.

"I only have a quarter. A soda at this joint costs a dollar. That's a rip-off."

"Maybe that's their way of paying for the exhibits," I suggested as I rummaged in my backpack for some change. "The entrance fee is so low that they have to make up for it by charging a dollar for a Coke."

Alan emptied his backpack onto the table. "I've got half a stick of gum, one rubber band, my zoo key, ten pennies, two nickels, and a quarter."

Howie's pockets contained one quarter, an old movie ticket stub, several nails, his zoo key, a rabbit's foot, and a neon green yo-yo.

When I emptied my pack onto the table, it really got silly. A comb, three nickels, two quarters, my zoo key, a cat keychain, several pencils, and two erasers.

"What is this, a rummage sale?" Claudia asked, joining us at the picnic table.

"We're trying to come up with a dollar for a soda," I explained.

Claudia studied the pile of items and coins on the table. "It looks like you can buy one coke and three straws. And then make a great collage with the rest of that stuff."

Alan picked out the change. "I'll buy."

While he stood in line at the snack bar, Howie and I started gathering up the rest of our belongings.

Suddenly Claudia was tugging on my sweater. "There they are," she hissed. "Over there."

"Who?" I asked.

"The matching sweatsuit spies," Claudia replied.

We didn't get a chance to hear what they were saying because Dawn and the Arnold twins suddenly appeared.

"Look!" Carolyn cried in a voice that could shatter glass. "Those people are wearing matching outfits and they're not even twins."

Howie was the one who had noticed them in the first place, so he was as interested in their reappearance as we were. He grabbed the rest of his things and stuffed them back in his pockets. "Which way are they headed?" he asked loudly.

Claudia's face was frozen in a smile and she barely moved her lips as she said, "Right this way!"

The two people were having an intense discussion over some notes they'd made on a piece of paper.

Now all of the customers at the snack bar turned and stared at them.

"Very subtle," Dawn cracked. "Do you want to shout a little louder?"

"Howie, our soda's here," I said, changing the subject. "Let's drink it before the ice melts."

Alan, Howie, Dawn, and the twins sat down at the picnic table.

As Marilyn scooted onto our bench she said, "Those protester people are here again."

I nodded. "They're here every day."

"I guess these animals mean a lot to them," she said.

"I wonder how far they'll go," Dawn said, handing each of the twins a small carton of apple juice from her bag. "When we went through the front gate, I talked to one of them about the emu. He didn't seem the least bit surprised, or even upset, that one of the zoo animals had gotten out and was running free."

"Maybe he knew it was going to happen," I suggested. "He could have been part of the plot."

"What plot?" Howie asked.

"The plot to free the animals," I said. Then I turned to Dawn. "I hope you remember what he looks like. He could be a suspect."

Dawn nodded. "I'll write it down. Tall and thin with red moustache."

Claudia, who had gotten herself an ice-cream cone, finished it, and returned to the table. "Well, back to work," she said.

Alan, who had taken several sips of our shared Coke, stood up also. "Today I'm watching the emu. I think I'll take a look at how she handles the stress of glimpsing freedom and then having it ripped away from her."

"That sounds grim," I said. "Are you sure you wouldn't want to study the bears or seals?"

"Oh, no," Alan said with a sly smile. "Besides, I have a feeling I'm going to make some prize-winning observations today."

"What makes you think that?" Dawn asked, taking a sip of her own juice.

Alan wiggled his eyebrows. "That's for me to know and you to find out." He looped his backpack over one shoulder and sauntered off.

"Well, Howie?" I said, facing him. "Which do you want — the bears or the seals?"

"Bears," Howie replied, taking a final loud slurp of our soda. "I'm really starting to like those guys."

"Then I'll take the seals," I said, grabbing my backpack. "This should be fun. Catch you guys later."

Dawn waved good-bye. "Don't forget to check the bushes," she reminded me. "And watch for any suspicious people."

I gave her a thumbs-up. I had every intention of checking for berry bushes. In fact, I'd already decided to take the long way to the seals. That way I could have one more look at Edith the emu's pen.

Alan had a few minutes' headstart on me, but I fully expected to catch up with him at the emu pen. When I got there, though, he was nowhere to be seen, which was strange, since he had done that little eyebrow wiggle, saying he was going to be making some prize-winning observations about emus. I followed the fence along the entire perimeter of the emu enclosure. No Alan.

But I did discover something else. Where the emu fence bordered the primate area was a large cluster of bushes. *Red* berry bushes, to be exact. Some of the lower branches were quite near to the ground. I wondered if they were low enough to have been walked on. As I bent down to examine them more closely, several of the new employees in blue blazers went running by.

"We're over by the primates, base," one of them said into his walkie-talkie. "We're coming on the double to help with containment."

Something was up. I decided to follow them, to see what the commotion was about. The men hurried around the side of the primate enclosure, where Mojo and James were on display, then hurried down a sidewalk leading toward the African savannah exhibit.

I wondered if one of the elephants was having a problem. But no, the men hurried past the elephant barns and amphitheater, heading toward the giraffe house.

A crowd had already gathered. Several of the new security people were setting up a barricade with yellow sawhorses. Mrs. Wofsey was there, speaking to the onlookers in a steady, firm voice.

"Please, everyone, stay back," she ordered. "Giraffes may look harmless but if they become frightened or angry, they can be quite dangerous."

Two zookeepers appeared, holding long ropes which were loosely draped around the neck of the giraffe ambling along between them. She was about fourteen feet tall and towered above everyone. If I hadn't known the giraffe had escaped, I might have thought the three of them were out for an afternoon stroll.

"Here you are, Geraldine," Mrs. Wofsey said in a reassuring voice. "Back home, safe and sound."

Geraldine's eyes darted back and forth as she spied the large crowd milling behind the barriers. Her nostrils flared several times, but she made no attempt to kick or run. She waited patiently as the keepers opened the gate leading into the corral. Several other zoo-keepers were waiting for her inside with a bucket of oats. They used a long stick to lift the bucket up to the feeding trough, which was attached to a pole.

The moment Geraldine spied the food, she trotted into the corral. Instantly the gate was shut behind her and Mrs. Wofsey breathed a sigh of relief.

"Well, now, that's that," she said to the crowd. "I guess, since it was such a nice day, Geraldine thought she'd take herself out for a little stroll."

This drew a chuckle from the crowd.

"Rest assured, folks," Mrs. Wofsey continued, "the Bedford Zoo will not let an incident like this happen again."

But how will they stop it? I thought. Already two animals had been set free. How many more would escape before they discovered *whodunnit*? As the crowd dispersed, I noticed something odd. Marilyn Arnold was standing by herself near the gate to the giraffe house. She was looking guiltily over one shoulder. If she weren't so young, I might have thought she had something to do with the escape. I decided I'd better keep an eye on her.

"That was pretty exciting, wasn't it, Marilyn?" I said, joining her at the gate.

Marilyn nodded sadly. Her chin was quivering as if she were about to cry.

"What's the matter?" I asked.

She pointed to the giraffe, who had devoured the oats and was now looking over the fence at us. "Geraldine looks so sad," Marilyn murmured. "I wish she didn't have to live in that cage."

I draped my arm over Marilyn's shoulder. "I wish that, too. But these people seem very kind. Look, the zookeeper is scratching her behind the ear with that long brush. Geraldine seems to like it."

Marilyn shrugged. "Maybe. But it still is sad."

"Come on, let's go find Dawn," I said. "I'm sure she is wondering where you are."

"Dawn and Carolyn are watching the monkeys. I just couldn't go there."

"We'll walk back," I said, already guiding her to the primate enclosure. "Then you and I can wait outside."

We ran into Howie and Alan on the way.

"I looked for you at the emu pen," I said to Alan. "But you weren't there."

"Uh, I was with Howie," Alan explained. He seemed very nervous. "We decided to watch the seals. They were tossing a ball around and being really squirrelly."

"It's too bad you missed all the excitement," I said. "One of the giraffes escaped from her cage."

"What?" Howie gasped. "Did they have to tie her down and sedate her with one of those tranquilizer guns? That must have taken a lot of guys."

"I think you've been watching too many safari movies," I said with a laugh. "Two of the keepers just walked her back into the corral. I guess they were lucky she didn't fight. Mrs. Wofsey said giraffes can be pretty fierce if they're upset."

"Marilyn!" Dawn cried, hurrying to join us. Her face was red from running. "Where have you been? Carolyn and I have been looking for you everywhere."

"I was watching the giraffe," Marilyn replied.

Dawn turned to me and said stiffly, "Would you watch Carolyn for a moment? Marilyn and I need to have a very serious talk."

She took Marilyn by the hand and led her to the nearest empty bench. I couldn't hear what Dawn was saying but I could guess from their body language. Dawn's face was tense and she was talking a mile a minute, while Marilyn stared down at her hands, her head bent. Every few moments Marilyn nodded. Dawn was making it very clear to Marilyn that slipping off by herself to explore the zoo was not acceptable.

Suddenly Howie nudged me with his elbow. Well, nudged is not exactly the right word. Jabbed, is more like it. "The weirdos are back," he hissed.

The weirdos — the couple with the cameras and the matching gray-and-red sweatsuits — weren't just back, they were standing less than six feet from us, in front of the primate enclosure. They were scribbling furiously on their notepads.

A light bulb went on in my head. This couple was at the zoo when the emu escaped and now here they were again, just moments after the giraffe escaped.

I decided to do a little investigating. Casually I pulled my own notebook out of my pack and, pretending to take notes, stood directly behind the woman.

She'd written strange words such as "papio," "colobus," and "hylobates" on her notepad. Beside each word was a dollar amount.

Very odd. The words looked as if they might be Latin but I had no idea what they meant. The dollar figures, however, were in the thousands. One thing was certain — whatever they were writing about was worth a lot of money.

That afternoon I returned home with plenty

to think about. Alan and Howie hadn't been where they were supposed to be. Two people in matching sweatsuits were a bit *too* interested in the gibbons. And the animals? Well, someone was definitely setting the animals free.

CHAPTER 9

Thursday

My sister Becca is totally into saving Babar. And she has managed to get most of her friends to help. I was supposed to watch just Squirt and Becca on Thursday, but once we started working on the Free Babar project, I felt like I was baby-sitting for the entire neighborhood.

Jessi's aunt had scheduled her to sit for her brother and sister after school. She hadn't been gone five minutes before the doorbell rang.

"I'll get it," Becca called, running to the door. "That should be Charlotte. I asked her to come over to help Free Babar. I hope you don't mind."

Becca looks like a miniature version of Jessi, except her eyes aren't quite as dark and her legs aren't as long. She's a sweet girl, kind and thoughtful and a little shy.

Charlotte, who used to be *very* timid and shy until Stacey helped her become more outgoing, marched confidently through the front door and into the living room. She smiled at Becca, revealing a dimple in each cheek.

"I'm all ready to work," she said, patting her kitty-cat backpack. The kitten on the pack matched the kitten on the headband holding back her chestnut-brown hair.

"Come on." Becca gestured for Charlotte to follow her. "We'll work at the coffee table."

"I think we should write Free Babar letters," Charlotte said as she laid some pink stationery on the coffee table. She pulled a pencil box decorated with pink bunnies out of her pack and opened it. "I've got purple, red, and blue pens. We can write the letters in one color, then every time we mention Babar's name, we can decorate it with the other colors."

Jessi nodded her approval. "That will make his name stand out. But who are we writing to?"

"The people at Valley Park Shopping Center, where Babar is being held prisoner," she said. "I think they should know how we feel, and why freeing Babar is so important."

Becca knelt by the coffee table. "People use letters to raise money, too. Maybe we could write to our friends' parents and ask them to help."

Squirt, who has been going through the terrible twos even though he's not two yet, grabbed Charlotte's pens and ran toward the kitchen with them.

"Squirt!" Becca squealed. "Bring those back."

Jessi remembered the last time Squirt had gotten his hands on nonwashable pens. He'd drawn purple and green squiggles on the walls and the furniture. He'd even scribbled on the toilet seat. She wasn't about to let that happen again.

"Hold on, Squirt!" Jessi grabbed him before he could crawl under the kitchen table. She peeled his fingers off of Charlotte's fancy pens and said, "I have some other pens, just for you."

"Mine!" Squirt reached stubbornly for the pens.

Jessi sighed and tried to explain things to him calmly. "Those are for Charlotte and Becca. I have some very special pens for you, with much more fun colors. Like pink and orange — "

"Owange?" Squirt's eyes lit up. "Mine!"

Jessi hurried to get the markers and some extra large pieces of construction paper for Squirt to scribble on. While she was in the other room, the doorbell rang again.

"I'll get it," Becca called to her. "It should be Haley Braddock."

Jessi grabbed the markers from a shelf in the kitchen and hurried to the front hall. "How many more people are you expecting?" Jessi asked, as Becca let Haley in.

"I think that's it," Becca answered, leading Haley into the living room. "But I'm not sure."

"Look, Becca," Jessi said, as pleasantly as possible, "if anyone calls, tell them to come back another day. I'm afraid we won't have enough paper or pens to write with."

"Don't worry," Haley Braddock said cheerily. "I brought my own stationery. It has my name on it. And I have some extra pens, too. Here are my supplies." Haley held up a slender box of lavender stationery and a plastic zipper bag of pens. "I already wrote my first letter. Want to hear it?"

Jessi was impressed. The girls really had been working on the Free Babar project. "Sure, Haley. Read it to us."

Haley opened her stationery box and carefully lifted out the top sheet. "Dear Mr. or Mrs. Shopping Center Owner." She lowered her paper and explained, "I didn't know the person's name so I thought that would cover everything."

"Sounds good," Jessi said, with an encouraging smile.

"We all need a nice home where we can be happy," Haley continued. "If where we live is not nice, then we will be sad. Babar needs his own place to be happy. It's not fair to keep an elephant in a shopping mall. He needs trees and grass like his home in Africa. Animals have feelings. Babar's feelings are hurt. Help make him happy. It would make me very happy if you did. I will help you in any way that I can. Sincerely, Haley Braddock. Age nine. Stoneybrook Elementary."

Becca and Charlotte applauded when Haley finished reading her letter, while Squirt banged his hands on the table.

"That's telling them," Becca said. "Can I look at your letter when I write mine?"

Haley blushed and handed Becca the piece

of paper. "Sure. You can copy it exactly if you want."

Charlotte Johanssen was not to be outdone. She quickly signed her name at the bottom of her stationery and then said, "Would you like to hear my letter? This one is to the mayor."

"Mine!" Squirt suddenly appeared from around the side of the couch, grabbed Charlotte's letter, and ran for the kitchen again.

Once more Jessi chased after him. This time Charlotte was right behind her.

"Squirt!" Charlotte cried. "Please don't wrinkle my letter. I'll have to do it all over again."

"No!" Squirt crawled under the kitchen table and then squirmed beneath the chair. The letter was now a crumpled sheet of paper clutched tightly behind his back. He giggled and a long string of drool ran down his chin.

"I'm sorry, Charlotte," Jessi said as she inched slowly toward her little brother. "Squirt thinks this is a game."

Charlotte knelt on the floor and looked at Jessi's brother with her big dark eyes. "Oh, Squirt. That makes me sad."

He lurched out from under the chair and shoved the letter into Charlotte's lap. "No cwy. No cwy."

Charlotte took the crumpled piece of paper and gave Squirt a hug. "Thanks for giving it back. I guess I can use it as a guide for my next letter."

Jessi smiled warmly at Charlotte. "Thank *you* for being so understanding, Charlotte. I'll make sure Squirt stays away from your work from now on."

For the next hour, Becca, Haley, and Charlotte worked diligently on their letters. Jessi tried to keep Squirt away from the table by reading him stories. She chose, appropriately enough, some Babar books, which entertained everyone.

When the girls tired of writing, they went into the kitchen for a snack of yogurt and fruit. Jessi took that opportunity to fill them in on the plans for the walkathon.

"You know, Kristy and her stepfather, Watson, have made arrangements to let us do a walkathon," Jessi said, as she passed out apple and orange slices on paper towels. "The course will be four miles long, and it will wind in and out of the neighborhoods, with the final stretch going right down Main Street to the courthouse steps."

"What can we do to help?" Becca asked, taking a bite of her apple slice.

"We need to design pledge sheets for you kids to take around."

"We can do that," Charlotte said. "You just need the name of the walkathon at the top and little lines for people's names and addresses. You also need a line for how much they're willing to pay per mile."

Jessi took a spoonful of her yogurt. "Kristy suggested we ask for a dollar a mile. If every kid walks the full four miles, that could really add up."

"Does the walkathon have a name?" Charlotte asked.

Jessi smiled. "Kristy named it the Elephant Walk."

"The Elephant Walk!" Haley giggled. "I love it. We could dress up in elephant costumes and lead the parade."

"That would be awfully cute," Jessi said, smiling at the thought of the girls in elephant costumes.

Charlotte, who is *not* a big fan of dressing up and being silly in front of people, said, "Why don't you and Becca be the elephants, and I'll design the pledge sheets?"

"If you draw up the pledge sheets," Jessi said, "I'll bet Watson Brewer could have them copied for us. After Kristy talked to him, he said he would do anything he could to help out."

"While Charlotte does the pledge sheets, we can work on our costumes. Don't you have some gray tights we could wear?" Becca asked Jessi.

"I'm sure I do," Jessi replied. (Actually, she must have at least two dozen pairs of tights and as many leotards.) "Some of my pink pairs are so faded they look almost gray. And Mama could probably help you sew on the ears and trunk. I think she has some gray felt left over from the cat costume she made me a few years ago for Halloween."

The kids hurried to finish their snacks, anxious to start on their new projects. Jessi stayed in the kitchen and washed Squirt's face and hands, as well as the area where he'd been sitting. "I don't know how you do it," she said, dabbing at his face with a warm washcloth. "But you have managed to get yogurt on every part of the table, your chair, and the floor all the way to the wall."

Squirt smiled and another string of drool dripped onto his T-shirt.

"Very attractive," Jessi said, swiping at it with a wet washcloth.

Ding-dong!

Jessi set Squirt down and hurried to the front hall to answer the doorbell. Becca was already there, with her back pressed against the door, smiling sheepishly. "Remember when I said I didn't invite any other kids?"

"Yes." Jessi raised an eyebrow.

"Well, I forgot."

Jessi peered through the peephole in the

door. Vanessa and Margo Pike, Sara Hill, and Corrie Addison were standing in a tight cluster on the front porch. Jessi looked down at her sister. "So you forgot, huh? There are four more kids out there. What did you do? Make an announcement over the PA system?"

Becca shook her head. "No, I just mentioned it at recess."

Jessi gasped. "I can't take care of that many kids."

Ding-dong!

The girls on the front porch were growing impatient.

"Aren't you going to open the door?" Becca asked.

"I'm thinking," Jessi replied, "of what to say."

"How about, come on in?" Becca suggested.

"Not to them," Jessi shot back. "To Aunt Cecelia, when she sees that I've been baby-sitting for eight kids. She'll have a heart attack."

Jessi really didn't want to tell the girls to go home. Especially since they'd come to help Free Babar. But she was feeling overwhelmed by the number of kids she was suddenly supposed to be responsible for.

Luckily for Jessi, her aunt's car pulled into the driveway then, and the crisis was resolved.

Except for one thing. While Jessi and Becca

were talking in the front hall, Squirt found the half-empty yogurt carton. He emptied it onto the floor and was busy practicing his skating when Jessi's aunt walked through the door. What a day!

CHAPTER 10

"The adult emu generally weighs about one hundred and twenty pounds," Alan was saying. "He stands on three toes. His wings are short and nearly hidden under his tail feathers. The main shaft and second shaft are the same length so it looks like he has two layers of feathers. The emu eats hundreds of caterpillars and grasshoppers which he keeps in his mouth until it forms a big ball about the size of a baseball, then he swallows it. The emu doesn't sweat, he pants to stay cool. He also does quite a bit of yawning. When he sleeps, he lies with his head stretched out along the ground. He doesn't take water baths, but he does like to give himself a dirt bath. The dirt sops up the excess oil and gets rid of parasites and ticks."

Logan and I listened as Alan read from his observation book on Saturday afternoon. He was very proud of what he had recorded.

"You learned all that from watching the emu pen?" Logan asked, narrowing his eyes suspiciously.

"I didn't just watch," Alan corrected him. "I *observed*. Big difference."

"Well, I made some interesting observations about gorillas," Logan said, turning his back on Alan and focusing on me.

"Yeah, he observed that they look a whole lot like some of his relatives," Alan joked.

"They may look like my family," Logan retorted. "But they act like yours. Especially when they're picking fleas out of each other's hair."

Logan pretended a flea had jumped from Alan to him. He swatted at it and returned the imaginary dead flea to Alan's head.

"That's so funny I forgot to laugh," Alan said, staring angrily at Logan.

"Okay." I waved my hands in front of their faces. "Fun time is over. Time for us to regroup and go our different ways."

Alan and Logan continued to glare at each other. I had to grab Alan's arm to pull him away from Logan. "Come on, Alan. I want to hear more about your observations. I'm amazed at how detailed they are. When I was watching Edith, all she did was sleep, take a drink of water, and sleep some more."

Alan was distracted. He murmured, "If

you're going to win this game, you have to do a little more than just sit and stare."

"It's not a game," I reminded him.

"You're right." Alan glanced over his shoulder at the spot where Logan had been standing. "It's war."

"Oh, brother!" I groaned. Every time I saw Logan or Alan I could feel my shoulders tightening and a knot forming in my stomach. This had to change. Sooner or later I was going to develop an ulcer.

My group had agreed to meet at the emu enclosure. Howie was there waiting for us when Alan and I arrived. He wasn't even facing the pen. His attention was glued to a group of girls from our school who were watching the gorillas playing outside in the area next to the emu enclosure.

"Yo, Howie," Alan called, cupping his hands around his mouth. "Watcha staring at? *Girrrlls?*"

Sometimes boys can act so geeky.

The group of girls Howie had been staring at moved on, and I spotted Jessi and Matt Braddock standing in front of the cage.

At the BSC meeting on Friday, all we had talked about was the zoo mystery. What would happen next? Would we be able to unearth new clues? That was when Jessi had the brilliant idea of bringing Matt Braddock to the zoo to talk to Mojo in American Sign Language. She thought Matt could ask Mojo if she knew who freed the animals, and we all thought it was a terrific plan. So Jessi talked to the Braddocks and arranged a visit for Matt.

I left Alan and Howie at the emu pen and went over to talk to Jessi and Matt. I only know a little bit of sign language. For instance, "Hi, how are you?" and, "I'm hungry" and "time for bed." (Matt did teach us how to sign "Twinkle, Twinkle, Little Star" but that doesn't come in handy very often.)

Anyway, I said hi to Jessi and signed hello to Matt. I also asked him how he was doing. He smiled a big ear-to-ear grin and answered me.

"Matt can't wait to talk to Mojo," Jessi translated.

Mojo, a two-hundred-and-fifty-pound female gorilla, was leaning on a rock near the front of her enclosure, idly munching on browse. Browse is a leafy plant that the zoos put in cages so the animals can eat but not gain weight. (Kind of like humans eating carrots for a snack instead of crackers.) I learned this from the information kiosk.

James was lying on his back in a corner, taking a nap in the afternoon sun. He was a huge silverback male, and weighed over four hundred pounds.

Matt and Jessi tried to position themselves in front of Mojo, so that the gorilla could easily see Matt's signs. Matt caught Mojo's eye and signed *hello*.

Hello, Mojo answered casually.

Matt asked Mojo if the food she was eating was good.

Mojo signed *good*.

At that moment the small door in the back of the cage opened and Mr. Chester peered into the enclosure. He was holding two trays of food. Mojo instantly sat up.

I turned to Jessi. "I guess it's feeding time."

Jessi nodded. "It looks like those guys are eating extremely large TV dinners."

Matt couldn't hear us but it didn't matter. All of his attention was focused on Mojo. He signed the question, *Who let the emu out of her pen?*

Mojo looked sideways at Mr. Chester and the big metal trays full of food, and didn't answer.

Matt asked the question again.

This time Mojo responded with the word for *food*.

Matt's shoulders slumped. He turned to Jessi and signed, "It's not working."

Jessi patted him on the shoulder and signed back, *It's okay. She wants to eat.* She looked at me and said, "Maybe it's hard for Mojo to think when it's her lunchtime."

Mr. Chester was just about to enter the cage when he spotted something behind us and frowned. He slid the metal door shut. Moments later he appeared around the side of the building, and shouted, "Hey, you boys, what are you doing?"

He was talking to Alan and Howie, of course. They were by the berry bushes. "Just standing here," Alan replied. "Why?"

Mr. Chester pointed at the twig full of berries Howie held in his hand. "It looked as if you were going to feed the gorillas some of those berries."

Howie looked at his hand guiltily and dropped the berries. "I didn't even know I'd picked this. I wasn't thinking. Honest."

Mr. Chester bent down and picked up the twig. "These would not be good for the gorillas," he said sternly. "I don't want to see you touching those bushes again. Understand?"

"Yes, sir," Howie replied. "I won't."

Mr. Chester gestured for the boys to move onto the sidewalk. "And stay on the walkways, that's what they're here for."

Alan and Howie took two giant steps forward. Once Mr. Chester was satisfied that they weren't going to return to the bushes, he

112

hurried back to the side of the building.

Mojo and James had seen their lunches coming and were upset when they didn't arrive. They were now pounding on the metal door.

"I'm coming! I'm coming!" we heard Mr. Chester call. He slid the little metal door open and then unlocked the gate, slipping the two trays inside.

Mojo took her tray to a rock. We watched her daintily sift through the vegetables, sampling each one.

"Let's get out of here," Alan murmured.

I didn't blame them for wanting to leave. Mr. Chester had sounded pretty harsh. If he had said those things to me, I probably would have cried.

"Look, why don't you two watch the bears," I said, "and I'll take the seals. And we'll all come back here to the emu pen a little later."

"Fine," the boys muttered.

Logan, who had been at the snack bar near the seal pool, saw me as I came around the bend and ambled over to see what I was up to.

"Popcorn?" He held his bag out to me.

"Thanks. Popcorn is a lot more appetizing than what they're eating," I said, pointing to the fish the keeper was tossing to the seals.

"How's it going with Howie and the jerk?" Logan asked, tossing a handful of popcorn into his mouth.

"Logan?" I stared down at the rail surrounding the seal pool. "I wish you wouldn't call Alan a jerk. He may act like one sometimes but it doesn't help when you provoke him."

Logan looked hurt. "He's not exactly Mr. Nice Guy to me."

"I know that. It's just that things have become so tense between you two, it makes me feel awkward. This project should be fun — observing the animals and picking up behind-the-scenes information about a zoo. But instead of enjoying it, all I do is worry about what's going to happen when you two see each other."

Logan's face filled with concern. "Gee, Mary Anne, I didn't know you felt that way. I guess you're right. This competition thing has gone a little too far."

"A *little*?" I raised one eyebrow.

"All right, a *lot* too far."

"I mean, I'd like to win," I told him. "I could really use that extra credit. We all could. But I won't resent it if your team wins."

Logan put his left hand on his heart and held up his right hand. "You have my word that I won't be angry if your team wins either

— although it would be nice if my team won. But to show you I mean it, I promise from this moment forward to try to be nice to Alan."

I laughed. "Well, you don't have to go overboard. Knowing Alan, he'll think something's up. He'll probably say you're trying to kill us with kindness so you can do something tricky behind our backs."

Logan laughed and nodded. "You're right. He would think that."

"I have to admit I thought Alan was going to be a real goof-off on the project, but it's amazing how much it matters to him. Look at all of those great observations he made about the emu."

"Yeah." Logan cocked his head. "He did have more stuff than I've been able to get on the gorillas. I mean, it's really incredible how detailed his stuff was."

Aroo! Aroo!

The biggest seal in the pool had clambered on top of one of the rocks and was barking at the keeper, a blond man in green work clothes and a yellow slicker. The keeper chuckled and said to the small crowd who had gathered to watch feeding time, "Sparky never lets me get away with anything."

The man dug in the pocket of his raincoat and produced one final fish. He tossed it high in the air. Sparky dove off his rock and caught the fish midair, hitting the water with a tremendous splash.

The crowd's applause jarred something in my memory. "Feeding time. That means it's two o'clock. Mrs. Wofsey's video presentation about Mojo and sign language is at two. Come on, Logan," I said, pulling him away from the seal pool. "We don't want to miss it."

Our route to the visitors' center took us past the primate area where I saw the two people in matching sweatsuits huddled together.

"Look," I hissed to Logan. "Those — those *spies* are here again." I'd told Logan about our mystery. "I wonder what they're up to."

"Let's swing a little closer," he said. "Maybe we'll hear something."

Logan, who was holding my hand, suddenly swerved left and we nearly crashed directly into the back of the couple. Fortunately they were too wrapped up in what they were talking about to notice us.

"I'd say a gibbon costs at least eight-and-a-half thousand," the man was saying. "That is if the market is good."

"A macaque could be even higher," the woman replied. "And gibbons do make nice pets in their preteen years."

Logan and I pulled away from the couple.

"They're talking about how much monkeys cost!" I gasped.

"Yeah, and selling them as pets," Logan whispered back. "This is too weird."

Wrapped in our thoughts about what we'd just heard, Logan and I walked the rest of the way to the visitors' center. When we reached it, the presentation had already begun.

CHAPTER 11

"Now before I introduce our guest speaker, I'd like to make one last announcement."

Mrs. Wofsey was standing at a podium on the small stage at the visitors' center, which was packed with students and visitors. The benches were filled so Logan and I stood at the back.

"Next weekend we're throwing a 'Good-Bye, Gorillas' party for Mojo and James," Mrs. Wofsey said. "All of you eighth-graders from Stoneybrook Middle School are invited. Please feel free to bring your friends and families. It should be great fun."

Logan leaned over and whispered, "I wonder what kind of food they'll serve — carrots and browse? Or do gorillas like chocolate cake?"

"Everybody likes chocolate cake," I whispered back.

"And now it is my great pleasure to introduce a pioneer in primate studies," Mrs. Wofsey said. "She has been exploring nature ever since she first went to work for the American Museum of Natural History in New York at age seventeen. Please give a warm welcome to Dr. Arden P. Wordsworth."

Arden P. Wordsworth? The name sounded so old-fashioned that I half-expected to see an old lady totter out. Instead a tanned, athletic woman hopped onto the stage. I guessed she was around fifty but she moved more like somebody my age.

"Greetings, everyone," she said. "I'm here today to talk about two very good friends of mine, Mojo and James."

"Mojo and James were born at the Huntington Animal Park," Dr. Wordsworth continued. "They have never lived in the wild and have always been accustomed to having humans around."

Dawn raised her hand.

"Yes?"

"Don't you feel it's cruel to keep animals penned up like that?" she asked.

Miss Wordsworth smiled. "If I thought it was cruel, I would never be associated with it. However, I do take your point that animals like to have their freedom, as do we all. But let me ask you this — do you have a pet?"

"I don't," Dawn replied. "But my stepsister has a cat."

"Do you feel it's cruel to keep a cat penned up in your house?"

"No," Dawn said. "But that's different. A cat is small."

"Let's put this in perspective," Dr. Wordsworth said. "Most of us assume that any captive animal longs to be free. But animals can't always do as they like in the wild. Strict limits are put upon them by the seasons, their territorial status, and the relative richness of their habitat." She paused, then said with a grin, "I'm sorry, I'm starting to sound like a professor. Mojo's and James's home at the San Diego Zoo is a painstaking recreation of their African habitat, a full three acres. They're both lowland gorillas who, in the course of a normal day, would probably travel no further than half a mile. They're safe, warm, and well-fed. Besides spending time with each other, Mojo and James spend several hours a day in structured play, where new challenges are constantly introduced to them. This is where Mojo first learned sign language. James never really picked it up, by the way. Occasionally he imitates Mojo, but that's all it is — imitation."

"I thought I saw him signing to Mojo," I whispered to Logan. "That explains it."

"Before I show you the film, I would like to say that Mojo's great strides in communication would probably not have been possible if it weren't for the breakthrough studies of Dr. Penny Patterson, who first worked with a little gorilla named Koko at the San Francisco Zoo. Koko learned to sign four words in 1972. By the time she was seven, Koko counted six hundred and forty-five signs in her vocabulary, which she used to ask for presents, tell jokes, and express her feelings." Dr. Wordsworth waved at the back of the room. "Could someone start the video, please?"

"Mr. Chester was going to run our video for us," Mrs. Wofsey said, as she fiddled with the machine, "but I'm afraid he's not here. I'll need a few moments to make sure I'm pushing the correct buttons."

The delay gave me a chance to look around the room. I noticed that neither Alan nor Howie was in the audience.

Thunk.

The exit door slammed shut and Mr. Chester hurried into the room and rushed to Mrs. Wofsey. "I apologize for being late," he said. "But we seemed to be short-handed at feeding time. I had to feed the seals."

"That's quite all right." Mrs. Wofsey smiled stiffly. "Take a moment to catch your breath, and then we'll begin the video."

The door at the back slammed again and one of the new security guards rushed in. He stood near Logan and me, gesturing frantically. "Mrs. Wofsey? Mrs. Wofsey, please, I need to talk to you."

Mrs. Wofsey nodded. "All right, folks," she announced, "on with the show." She dimmed the lights, turned up the volume, then hurried to talk to the guard.

"What is it, Mike?"

"One of the gates in the primate enclosure — the gibbons' gate," the guard whispered, loudly enough so that Logan and I could hear. "I found it standing wide open."

"Oh, dear." Mrs. Wofsey reached for her walkie-talkie. "How many got loose?"

"None. Luckily, it was so close to feeding time that the gibbons were still eating and didn't feel like leaving."

"What's that?" Mr. Chester asked, joining the two. "We've had another escape?"

Only a few people in the back besides Logan and me could have overheard the guard's conversation with Mrs. Wofsey. But Mr. Chester's voice carried, and a few people in the audience turned to look.

"No," Mrs. Wofsey whispered loudly in the direction of the audience. "There has been no escape."

"What's going on?" Mr. Chester hissed.

"This is the third escape in a week."

Mrs. Wofsey glanced nervously at Dr. Wordsworth, who had heard everything, too. "Please, lower your voice," she said to Mr. Chester.

"How can these things be happening?" he continued.

Mrs. Wofsey shook her head. "I don't know. I've doubled our security force and patrolled the grounds myself."

"Well, you're the one in charge here," Mr. Chester reminded her. "If an animal escapes and someone gets hurt we'll know who to blame."

Mrs. Wofsey, who looked embarrassed, pursed her lips. "Thank you for reminding me. I suppose you think that if you were in charge, this wouldn't have happened."

"If I were in charge, *none* of the escapes would have occurred," Mr. Chester snapped back. "I'm going to go check the cage locks now." With those final words he spun and marched out of the auditorium.

In spite of the commotion, everyone was able to turn their attention back to Dr. Wordsworth and the video. After it was over, those of us who'd overheard Mr. Chester rushed out to the primate enclosure. I don't know what we expected to find, since the gibbons hadn't escaped. I guess we just wanted to visit the scene of the crime.

The gibbons' cage was next to the gorillas'. Logan and I watched some gibbons lazily roll a red ball around the cage.

Logan snapped his fingers. "Remember that couple? They were talking about how much a gibbon costs."

"I know," I said. "I've been thinking about them ever since that guard burst in with his announcement. But if they opened the cage, why didn't they take the gibbons?"

Logan shrugged. "Maybe someone, like that guard, happened to come along before they had the chance."

I watched the ball roll back and forth between the gibbons and then I noticed a purplish stain on the concrete just outside of the gibbons' door. "Logan, look! Berry stains."

"What?"

"There are berry stains near the gibbons' cage. They stop just at the door. There were berry stains inside the emu's cage when she was freed."

Logan still looked confused. Then I realized he hadn't been told about my berry discovery.

"I think the person who freed Edith, and unlocked the gibbons' cage door, stepped in red berries." I pointed to the berry bushes between the gorillas' cage and the emu enclosure. "That bush's branches are awfully low to the ground. And, now that I think about it, Alan and Howie were standing in those bushes just this morning."

Logan opened his mouth to speak, then smiled. "I was just about to say something rotten like, I might have known Alan would be involved, but I remembered that I promised to be nice."

"Good." I patted his shoulder. "Keep remembering that."

A group of students standing in front of the gibbons' cage soon migrated to Mojo's and James's area, where Dr. Wordsworth was now conducting an impromptu question-and-answer session.

"Does Mojo communicate with just one person?" Jessi Ramsey was asking. "Or can she talk to anyone who uses American Sign Language?"

"Mojo can speak with anyone," Dr. Wordsworth replied. "Many hearing-impaired people visit the Huntington Animal Park just for that reason."

Jessi gestured to Matt Braddock who stood beside her. Signing as she spoke, she explained, "My friend uses ASL, and he'd like to ask Mojo a few questions."

"Go right ahead." Dr. Wordsworth stepped back and watched as Matt tried to talk to Mojo.

Do you know who freed the emu? Matt asked the gorilla.

Mojo answered *Yes.*

Matt turned to Jessi, his face flushed with excitement. *She says she knows who freed the emu!* he signed.

Jessi grinned and signed back, *I know. Ask her who did it.*

Matt signed the question, and we all held our breaths, waiting for Mojo's reply. I knew enough ASL to understand the answer.

"Food," I said, turning to Logan. "That's what she said before. I wonder if she's hungry."

"Maybe she wants a treat before she'll answer," Logan suggested to the group at large.

Dr. Wordsworth shook her head. "Mojo doesn't normally ask for snacks. Maybe she is just hungry."

"Besides," Erica Blumberg added, "how would a gorilla know what an emu is?"

Matt and Jessi left the zoo, downcast. I guess we all felt a little disappointed. We were back to where we had started with berry stains as our only clue and the protestors and the people in sweatsuits as our only suspects. But it would have been pretty incredible if the gorilla *had* named the culprit, wouldn't it? Not only would Mojo be famous for knowing sign language, but she would have gone down in history as the first gorilla detective.

CHAPTER 12

Sunday.

The Baby Elephant Walk could have been a complete total disasstur. In fact if you had asked me sunday morning if I thoght it was going to hapen, I wold have said, "No way. Weer not reddy." But by noon Becca, Charlotte, Haley and the Pike Platoon pulled it off.

"I can't find my elephant ears!" Haley screeched from her room on Sunday morning. "Claudia, help."

Claudia had promised to sit for the Braddocks in the morning and then help supervise the Elephant Walk that afternoon. She hadn't realized that so much work would be left to the last minute.

Brrrring!

"I'll get it," Claudia shouted to Haley. "Check in the bottom drawer of your dresser. I think your mom said your costume was there." Claud picked up the phone and said, "Braddock residence."

"Hi, this is Vanessa. I collected the pledge sheets from most of the kids at school, but I don't know what to do with them."

Claudia, who was trying to prepare lunch for Haley and Matt while she spoke to Vanessa, reached for the freezer door and flung it open. "Let's see, Vanessa, I thought Kristy was supposed to be in charge of — macaroni and cheese!"

"Macaroni and cheese? I thought there wasn't going to be any food. Just the Free Babar buttons and T-shirts."

"Sorry, Vanessa." Claudia cradled the phone on her shoulder. "I'm trying to fix lunch here. Um, bring the sheets to the school playground at one o'clock and either Kristy or I will take them."

Ding-dong!

"It's like Grand Central Station here. Sorry, Vanessa. Gotta run," Claudia tossed the macaroni and cheese container on the counter, slammed the freezer door shut with one hand and hung up the phone with the other. Then she raced for the front door.

The Pike triplets and Sara and Norman Hill were standing on the front steps. They held a six-foot-long banner and were beaming at Claudia as she opened the door.

"What do you think?" Sara asked. "Doesn't it look great?"

Free Babar was printed in big letters and *Your coins count!* in smaller ones beneath it. All around the lettering were drawings of gold coins.

"It's terrific," Claudia said as she let the kids into the front hall. "But aren't you guys a little early? The parade doesn't start for over an hour."

"We painted the banner this morning," Sara Hill said, "and it's still not dry. My mom said we couldn't keep it in the house so we thought we'd bring it over here."

"That has wet paint on it?" Claudia gasped.

Byron Pike nodded. "Don't touch it. Look what happened to me." He stepped back to show Claudia the print of a large "B" on his T-shirt.

"Out!" Claudia shrieked. "Everybody, back

outside. Don't touch the walls or doors."

The five children hurried out the front door as Matt Braddock came bounding down the stairs. He grabbed Claudia's arm and pointed upstairs, where Haley was shouting, "I still can't find it. Help!"

Claudia gestured for Matt to stay with the kids out front. Then she ran up the stairs two at a time. Haley's room looked as if a tornado had hit it. Every drawer was pulled out of the dresser, and every shoe in her closet had been thrown into the room. In the middle of it all stood Haley, her chin quivering.

"It's all right," Claudia said, giving Haley a hug. "Your mom said the ears are here. I bet we'll find them. And if we can't, you're lucky that you have the world's greatest elephant ear-maker baby-sitting for you today."

Claudia and Haley picked up the room and Haley was right — the ears were nowhere to be found. However, they did collect a lot of dirty clothes, and while Claudia was taking them to the laundry room, she spied two pieces of gray felt stretched across the ironing board.

"I found them," she shouted to Haley. "Crisis solved!"

"Not quite," a voice answered from the front hall. Jessi Ramsey had heard that Claudia was at the Braddocks' and had come over to ask for help.

Claudia gave Haley the ears and hurried outside to check on Matt and the kids, passing Jessi on the way. "Is it dry yet?" she asked the kids.

Norman Hill held one hand over the banner and patted a letter. He held up a red palm to show Claudia.

"I guess not." Claudia sighed. She made a mental note to find a rag for Norman so he could clean his hand. In the meantime, Jessi was still waiting in the front hall, looking agitated.

"Sorry, Claudia," Jessi said. "It looks like you have your hands full, but I just remembered that I'm supposed to be in charge of music."

"Didn't you find a tape of the "Baby Elephant Walk?" Claudia asked.

"Oh, I have the tape, all right," Jessi said, "but I don't have anything to play it on, except a tiny little tape recorder. We need a huge boom box."

Claudia scratched her head. "Stacey has a great tape player with really loud speakers. We could put it in one of the kids' wagons and let them pull it."

Relief washed over Jessi's face. "Let's call her."

Claudia grabbed Jessi's elbow. "Aren't you forgetting something? We aren't speaking to Stacey."

"Oh, right." Jessi's shoulders slumped. "For a

minute there I thought our problem was solved."

Claudia saw the macaroni and cheese carton lying on the counter and hurried to stick it in the microwave. "It might still be," she said as they waited for the food to cook. "We just have to be clever about this. Maybe we can get someone else to ask Stacey."

"Like who?" Jessi asked. "One of the kids?"

"Why not?" Claudia said with a shrug. "We'll just ask Becca to ask Charlotte to ask Stacey if the kids can borrow her tape recorder for the parade."

"Do you think she'll let them?"

"Stacey adores Charlotte. Of course she will."

Jessi ran to the phone. For the next few minutes there was a flurry of activity as Jessi phoned Becca, who phoned Charlotte, and then called Jessi back to say she'd phoned Charlotte, who'd said she'd phone Stacey right away. Now Becca was waiting for Charlotte to call with Stacey's response.

Claudia took that opportunity to check on Haley, who had recovered from her crisis and now stood in front of the mirror in her mother's room, practicing elephant poses. Then Claud told Matt that lunch would soon be ready. She raced back into the kitchen to hurriedly put macaroni and cheese, apple sauce, and carrot sticks on two plates.

By the time the calls had been made, and lunch was served, and the children with the wet banner had decided to proceed to another house, Claudia was exhausted. She felt as if she'd run a marathon. Jessi's news didn't make her feel any better.

"Stacey said yes," Jessi said glumly. "On one condition — that she come with it. She even volunteered to pull the wagon at the front of the walkathon."

"Stacey leading the walkathon?" Claudia gasped. "Oh, Kristy will *love* that idea. No way! There's just no way!"

Jessi winced. "Too late. I told Becca to tell Charlotte to tell Stacey okay."

"You *what*? Oh, I wish it were Monday and we were going to school and the Elephant Walk were over."

Mrs. Braddock returned home a few minutes late, which gave Claudia no time to go home. She had to head straight for the playground, because the walkathon was set to start in fifteen minutes.

Claudia jogged through the groups of kids who were making their way to the starting line. She spotted Kristy's faded ball cap in the middle of a group of children to whom she was giving last-minute instructions.

"Hey, Claud," Kristy called cheerily. She proudly displayed one of the T-shirts that

Claud had designed and silk-screened. "What do you think?"

"It's you," Claudia said with a grin.

Kristy looped her stopwatch and whistle over her head. She was in full coach gear. "The kids showed me the banner. I think they did a good job."

"Just don't get within five feet of it," Claudia warned her. "The paint's still wet. Where's Dawn?"

"At the drugstore," Kristy replied. "She was supposed to help me pass out supplies, but she realized at the last minute that she had forgotten to buy film for her camera." Kristy gestured to the card table she'd set up on the playground. It was stacked high with baskets full of Free Babar buttons.

Claudia smiled approvingly. "It looks like the Pikes and their Badge-o-matic factory have been working overtime."

Kristy checked her clipboard. "I have the buttons. Haley and Becca will be in front in their elephant costumes — "

"Vanessa has the pledge sheets," Claudia interrupted.

"Good." Kristy nodded her head. "Watson and I drove the walkathon route this morning. The town really came through. They have bright orange sawhorses in place and are ready to cordon off the route."

"Mallory did a great job with the publicity," Claudia said. "Mom has been cutting the articles out of the paper. There were two tiny ones on Thursday and Friday and a really large spread in this morning's Sunday paper. The headline said KIDS CARE."

Kristy grinned. "I saw that. The photo was great, too. Eight Pike kids, showing off their buttons and T-shirts, with those ear-to-ear grins. You can almost hear them all shouting, *Cheese!*"

"And speaking of too cute for words . . ." Claudia pointed down the street. "Check out the little elephants coming our way."

Haley and Becca were in elephant costumes of gray tights, leotards, and hoods with big ears. They'd even found rubber elephant noses at Toy City.

Kristy checked her watch. "They're right on time. We're at T-minus four minutes and counting."

It was amazing how many children were participating in the Elephant Walk. I had offered to do a kid round-up, walking some of our clients' kids to the starting line. Jenny Prezzioso and the Arnold twins came with me to pick up Jamie Newton and Nina Marshall. The walkathon was supposed to be four miles long, but I'm sure we added another mile collecting all those children.

My group and I hit the playground seconds

before Charlotte Johanssen — and her friend — arrived. Charlotte was pulling a wagon behind her.

Kristy squinted into the afternoon sun. "Why is Charlotte pulling a wagon? For the fliers?"

Claudia gulped. She realized she hadn't broken the news to Kristy about the tape player. "Uh, no, we had some difficulty with the music. Jessi needed to borrow a tape player with really big speakers, so the Elephant Walk music could be heard."

"Oh." Kristy leaned forward, adjusting the bill of her cap. "But who's that with her?"

Jessi joined Claudia just then, and they answered together, "Stacey."

We were lucky that it was now T-minus one minute until the walkathon was supposed to begin, because from the look on Kristy's face, we could have had a major blow-out.

"We don't have enough time to change anything," she grumbled after checking her watch again. "I just hope she stays away from me."

Stacey did exactly that. She and Charlotte stood on the edge of the crowd until Kristy blew her whistle. Then Haley and Becca stepped forward in their elephant costumes and posed.

"They've been practicing that pose for two days," Jessi whispered to Claudia.

"I know." Claudia grinned. "When Haley wasn't panicking about her costume, she was practicing her pose and her bow. I guess she plans to do that when we hit the finish line."

Next, the banner kids took their places behind the elephants. Then Kristy gestured for Charlotte to bring the wagon forward, and Charlotte and Stacey moved into position. It was weird. Stacey and Kristy never even looked at each other. Jessi put her tape in the player and nodded to Kristy.

Kristy blew her whistle and shouted, "Let the Elephant Walk begin!"

The music blasted from the speakers and the kids in front began to march. I know it was supposed to be a walkathon, but it felt more like a parade, with the kids in costume and the music.

Kristy made sure that Charlotte and Stacey were far ahead and then she blew her whistle once more. The rest of us stepped out.

After all the stress Claudia had gone through in the morning, she ended up having fun. It was a sunny day, and the walkathon route was lined with friendly people anxious to help us Free Babar. They cheered and waved as the kids streamed by.

Here's the remarkable part of the day — every kid walked the entire four miles. A few, such as Claire Pike, covered the final few blocks on some other kid's shoulders, but they all made it!

CHAPTER 13

"I think we should talk to Mrs. Wofsey," Dawn said at our Wednesday BSC meeting. "She should know about those spies in the matching jogging suits."

"I'm with Dawn," Claudia agreed. "We've all watched them making lists with dollar amounts next to weird Latin words. And Logan and Mary Anne even heard them talking about how much a gibbon would cost."

I said, "And the next thing we knew, the cage was standing wide open."

"I'll talk to Mrs. Wofsey," Claudia volunteered. "I think she'd appreciate any clues we can give her."

"Speaking of clues," I said, "I can't stop thinking about those red berry stains. When the emu was freed the stains were both inside and outside the cage. With the gibbons, the berry stains stopped at the door. And with the giraffe, there were no stains at all. What do you think that means?"

Kristy, who hadn't really been part of our zoo investigation, offered a solution. "Maybe it just means that there are berry bushes near the emu and monkey cages, but not the giraffe."

I looked at Kristy. "Yeah. Maybe I'm trying to invent clues where there aren't any."

I went home that night more discouraged than ever. Nothing seemed to fit together.

But the next day, the pieces started to fall into place. It all began when I tried to use my zoo key in the bears' information kiosk. (I realized I'd listened to the emus' and the seals', but not the bears'.)

"It doesn't fit," I muttered. Several visitors who were standing near me at the bear exhibit overheard.

A man holding the hands of two little girls said, "I'd ask for my money back. They charge you for everything here."

I studied the key. "It's solid brass," I said to myself. "Not just painted gold." Then it hit me. "The missing zoo key!"

But how could I have gotten Mrs. Wofsey's key? I didn't remember dropping a key. Mrs. Wofsey lost hers a week and a half before on Friday. I must have had my own then, because

I used it to gather information about emus from the kiosk.

Shortly after, the emu was freed, so someone else must have had the key at that moment. The only other time my key was out of my backpack was when I dumped my pack onto the table to look for change for a soda. Alan and Howie both emptied their packs, too. That's when the key exchange must have happened.

Suddenly everything made sense. "Alan has the key!" I announced to the next group of strangers who had come to look at the bears. Normally I would have been embarrassed to have been caught talking to myself, but today it didn't matter. I had solved the mystery.

Alan Gray stole the zoo key. But why? Alan must have freed the emu so he could observe the emu on the run and win the contest. I stuck the key in my pocket and marched down the zoo sidewalk toward the emu enclosure, muttering, "No wonder he knew so much about emus. Nobody could get that kind of information watching from a park bench outside the fence. He was inside the emu's cage. And that also explains the berry stains. He was standing in the bushes."

Alan was sitting by the emu enclosure with his notepad open when I arrived. "We have to talk," I said bluntly.

"You look worried," Alan said, shutting the notebook. "You shouldn't be. With all the information I have here, we're sure to win the prize."

I looked directly into his eyes. "I *know* how you got your information."

He blinked nervously. "How?"

"You gave yourself away."

This time he swallowed before he spoke. "How did I do that?"

I put my hands on my hips and announced, "Alan, *I* have the key. The one you used to open the emu cage. We accidentally switched keys when we were pooling our money to buy a soda at the snack bar. But before that, you opened the cage and went inside. How do I know this?"

Alan shook his head, too confused to answer.

"Because there were berry stains inside the cage. You stepped on the berries outside the cage before you went inside to take a closer look."

"Berry stains . . . zoo key?" Alan finally muttered. "What are you talking about?"

"I'm talking about all of that information you picked up about the emu. Nobody could find it out just sitting on one of these benches. You had to have been up close and personal."

"That's not true," Alan snapped.

I threw my hands in the air. "Well, how else could you know so much about emus?"

Alan shot a nervous glance at his backpack, which was sitting open on the park bench. I followed his gaze and saw what he was looking at a large picture book titled *Australia's Flightless Bird, the Emu*.

"You — you found your information in a *book*?" I stammered.

"Shhhh!" Alan gestured for me to lower my voice. "I really need the extra credit. I wasn't observing anything from this bench. I mean, Edith just eats and sleeps. She never even comes near the fence."

"I know," I muttered. "It's kind of frustrating. But Mrs. Gonzalez told us we were strictly forbidden to use any information from a book. It has to be based on observation."

"Great." Alan's shoulders slumped. "This way we'll never beat Logan's group."

"Look, Alan," I said, "I think we have a lot of good information without that book. And you certainly didn't need to go into the emu's cage — "

"Hold on a minute!" Alan nearly shouted. "Don't you understand? I never went in the emu's cage. I never had the zoo key."

"Well, I didn't have it when the emu was freed," I shot back.

Alan squinted at me. "If you didn't have it, and I didn't have it, then — "

"Howie must have had it!" we both said at once.

"Come on." Alan tucked his notebook into his pack and looped it over one shoulder. "Let's find Howie."

"He must be at the seal pool," I said, "because I was watching the bears, and I didn't see any sign of him."

That's where he was, too. Howie was in the little grassy area across from the seal pool, lazily eating an ice-cream bar.

You should have seen his face when Alan confronted him. He turned so red the tips of his ears were blazing.

"Okay, okay. I found the key on the ground by the berry bushes," he confessed. "But I thought it was mine. I only realized it wasn't when I couldn't make it work in the information kiosk."

"So you tried the key on the emu's gate?" I asked.

He nodded. "But I only stepped into the pen. I mean, I wasn't there three seconds when I turned and ran." He looked at Alan and me and winced. "I guess I must have left the gate open. I felt terrible when I heard the emu had escaped."

Suddenly I remembered something. "I

should have known you weren't observing the bears that day. You told me they were all napping in the trees. Bears don't sleep in trees!"

Alan frowned at Howie. "Way to cover, dimwit!"

Howie narrowed his eyes. "You believed me."

Then Howie turned to me. "Hey, I may have accidentally freed the emu. But what about the giraffe and the gibbons? *You* had Mrs. Wofsey's key when all that happened."

"I was at the elephant painting exhibition when the giraffe got loose, and at the gorilla lecture when the gibbons' cage was left open." The boys stared at me, not quite convinced. "There were plenty of witnesses!" I cried.

"Time out!" Alan made a T with his hands. "I think we can safely say that none of us had anything to do with those two escapes. Which means there's a criminal running around with his — or her — own key."

My eyes widened. "You're right. Because we've had Mrs. Wofsey's lost key the entire time." I realized it was time to fill Howie and Alan in on the BSC's investigation. I told them everything we'd discovered and listed our key suspects. When I finished, Howie nudged Alan. "I think we should do some investigating of our own. You know, like scope out the zoo, and see who has a key, and who doesn't.

144

Maybe tail those two spies in the jogging suits some more."

Howie liked the idea. I decided to let them do their research. I was anxious to find Logan, Claudia, and Dawn, so I could tell them what I'd found out.

I bumped into the three of them in front of the visitors' center. But Claudia had news of her own, and could hardly wait to tell me about it.

"Mary Anne, I talked to Mrs. Wofsey this morning," she blurted out. "And those people in sweatsuits are agents, all right. But not spies. They're agents for an eccentric tycoon in New Hampshire. He wants to build a zoo on his estate. Mrs. Wofsey is helping them figure out how much it would cost to set one up."

"Whoa!" I said. "Wait till the animal rights activists hear about that!"

"Not to mention his neighbors," Logan joked. "Can you imagine? Instead of neighbors complaining about a dog barking, he'll be getting calls about his lion roaring."

"Or his gibbon shrieking," I said, laughing.

"Speaking of gibbons," Dawn said, "we still don't know who tried to set them free."

"Well, we do know who didn't do it," I said, "which is a start." Then I told Claudia and Logan how Howie had found Mrs. Wofsey's key and accidentally freed the emu. "Now I have the zoo key, so that means whoever did it has his or her own key."

"That propably eliminates the protestors," I said.

"And narrows it to zoo employees," Claudia said. "Like that guard, Mike, or Tim the vet — "

"Or Mr. Chester," I said. "Remember how unpleasant he's been to Mrs. Wofsey? He really seems to dislike her."

Logan pointed at me. "Remember the time we were watching the seals, when they were being fed?"

I nodded. "We talked about the competition, and then we went to Dr. Wordsworth's lecture."

"That was just before the gibbons' cage was found open," Logan said. "Now, do you remember what Mr. Chester said when he was late to the lecture?"

I nodded. "He said he had to feed the seals . . ." A light bulb in my brain suddenly went on. "But he *didn't* feed the seals, because you and I watched the blond guy with the moustache feed them fifteen minutes before."

"Exactly!" Logan cried.

"And the berry stains," I said, suddenly remembering the stains outside the gibbons' cage door. "Mr. Chester must have made them — "

"Because he was standing in the bushes," Dawn jumped in, "when he yelled at Howie and Alan about feeding the animals."

I was so excited I could hardly breathe. "We've got to tell Mrs. Wofsey right away. Like now."

Logan pointed to the office by the front gate. "Let's try her office."

We were in luck. She was in.

Logan, Claudia, Dawn, and I crowded into her tiny office and took turns telling our story. We told her about finding the zoo key, how the emu gate was accidentally left open, and especially about the berry stains and Mr. Chester's lie.

When we were finished, Mrs. Wofsey looked grim. She pursed her lips and shook her head for a long time before she spoke.

"It comes as no surprise that our culprit is Mr. Chester. You may or may not have noticed that there has been some tension between us. When I was hired for this position, he was resentful. He thought the job should have gone to him. He's done everything in his power to undermine my authority."

"What are you going to do?" Claudia asked. "Call the police?"

Mrs. Wofsey sighed. "Not just yet. You see, we really don't have anything concrete against him. All of the evidence is circumstantial."

"You need to catch him in the act," Logan said, nodding his head.

"But how?" Dawn asked.

Mrs. Wofsey stood up and moved to her bulletin board, where a big color photo of Mojo and James was displayed. "If Mr. Chester really wants to get me into trouble, he'll free the gorillas."

CHAPTER 14

G*ood-bye, Gorillas!* read the banner above the visitors' center. A large sandwich board outside welcomed the eighth-graders from Stoneybrook Middle School to the farewell party. Bouquets of green, silver, and purple balloons were everywhere.

That Saturday morning, Dawn and I had risen early. We'd wanted to go over our plans for the big stakeout.

After Mrs. Wofsey had expressed concern that Mr. Chester might try to free the gorillas, we had agreed the best time for him to do it would be the day of the good-bye party.

"Today's the day," Logan said as Dawn, Claudia, and I huddled outside the front gate that morning. "We'll have to be on our toes, never let Chester out of our sight, and report anything, I mean, *anything* strange."

"You got it," Alan said, joining our huddle.

Howie was right behind him. "Just tell us

what to do and we're there." He had arrived a little early so he could apologize to Mrs. Wofsey about leaving the emu pen open. After she let him off with a warning, he was even more excited than Alan was about catching the *other* suspect.

I realized I had forgotten to tell my friends that I'd invited Alan and Howie to help with our stakeout. I figured they were already involved because of the zoo key and the emu escape, and besides I'd filled them in on Mr. Chester. And well, they were my group partners. It would probably have been okay if they hadn't looked so ridiculous.

Howie had chosen to wear all black. I think he'd been watching too many spy movies. Alan was dressed in camouflage pants, T-shirt, and a camping cap.

"I thought hunting season was over," Logan cracked, looking at Alan. I shot Logan a warning look and he immediately backed off. "Thanks for helping out, Alan."

"No problem," Alan said. "I want to catch this Chester guy in the act."

I guessed that Alan's determination was fueled by the embarrassment he'd felt when Mr. Chester had yelled at him in the berry bushes.

"Okay, now that there are six of us," Logan

continued, "we can put two guards on the primate area, near the gorillas, one on Mr. Chester — "

"Which should change every fifteen minutes," I cut in. "Or he'll get suspicious."

"Right," Logan said. "The rest of us will patrol the area until it's our turn to watch Chester."

We made a list determining who would do what job first and in what order. Then I checked my watch. "It's ten o'clock. The party starts in half an hour. That gives us plenty of time to get to our positions."

"Now, the party lasts for an hour," Logan reminded us. "Then everyone is going to meet at the gorilla cage, where James and Mojo will be served banana cake."

"Gross," Alan said, grimacing. "I hope they don't want us to share it."

Logan chuckled. "Seriously. It would probably have gorilla slobber all over it. I've watched those guys eat. They lick everything first."

I was glad Logan was keeping his promise to be nice to Alan. It made everything so much more pleasant. Even spying on a possible criminal.

My first assignment was to stay by the visitors' center and watch the party guests, keeping an eye out for anyone looking suspicious. I liked this job because it let me attend the party. And boy, was it fun!

Mrs. Wofsey and her assistants had turned the center into a gorilla carnival. The pictures of the different animals had been replaced with life-size photos of Mojo and James at the Bedford Zoo. The room was lined with booths featuring a gorilla theme. At the far end of the room the video that Dr. Wordsworth had introduced to us was playing.

Kristy, who had missed the action during the week, brought her brother David Michael and her stepsister Karen to the party.

"I want to try the gorilla ring toss," Karen said, tugging on Kristy's arm. "Could I, please?"

"Of course." Kristy laughed. "We can try everything. And afterward we'll have a banana split at the Banana Boat snack bar."

My favorite display was the one titled *Gorilla My Dreams*. The zoo staff had made cardboard cutouts of two gorillas standing arm-in-arm, with a place between them for people to put their faces. A photographer with a Polaroid camera stood by, ready to take pictures. I made a mental note to bring Logan back here, if all went well.

I roamed the room, watching children color drawings of gorillas and make clay gorillas with a plastic mold. There were gorilla masks and even several guys dressed in gorilla suits in the crowd.

Mrs. Wofsey was in one corner talking to a group of students and their parents. She caught my eye and waved. I could tell she was worried about what might happen in the next hour. So I gave her a thumbs-up sign.

I checked my watch. Fifteen minutes had passed. Time for me to move to my new post by the gorilla cage. Before I left the building, I saw Mrs. Wofsey give a few instructions to the guys in the gorilla suits, then slip out the side door.

I passed Howie, who was taking over my position at the party. He had put on a pair of dark sunglasses and didn't even say hi as he walked by. He did pretend to scratch his head, and I noticed him wiggling a few fingers in my direction. I nearly laughed out loud.

Seconds later I heard feet pounding behind me. It was Logan. "This is it," he hissed. "I think Chester's making his move."

"Don't run," I replied. "He'll think something's up."

Immediately Logan slowed to a walk beside me. "Sorry, I got a little carried away," he said. "Claudia followed Chester to the employees' locker area, where he changed out of his blue blazer into green pants and a green shirt."

"So he'd look like the plant crew."

"You got it," Logan said. "He's wearing a hat and sunglasses. Claudia said she wouldn't have known it was him except for the way he walks, with his feet turned out like a duck."

"Way to go, Claud," I murmured. "Where's he now?"

"Alan spotted him at the golf carts. Chester made sure no one was around, then hopped in a cart. Alan said it looked as though he were heading for the primate enclosure."

Now *I* wanted to run. "I hope Dawn can handle it," I said. "She's the one on duty at the gorilla cage, right?"

Logan nodded. We were both jogging now. We couldn't help it. Chester was about to let the gorillas loose and we wanted to be there in time to stop him.

Dawn was at her post, pretending to listen to the information kiosk in front of the gorilla cage, when we arrived. She smiled and waved, then strolled over to greet us.

"He's in there," she said barely moving her lips.

I was holding a little plastic gorilla that I'd been handed at the party. I pretended to show it to Dawn, who acted as if it were the greatest prize she'd ever seen. "Have you seen Claud?" I asked.

Dawn nodded casually toward the emu enclosure, where Claudia, wearing a baseball cap and sunglasses, stood pretending to watch the big bird. She had slung a camera around her neck, and she raised it to one eye. Then she spun and faced the gorilla cage.

"A camera!" Logan whispered. "All right, Claud. We'll catch him in the act."

"Hold it." I clutched Logan's arm. "Who's that weird person next to Claudia?" We watched as a person in a baggy jumpsuit, a big floppy hat, and sunglasses bent down to look at one of the flowers lining the walkway.

"It's not Chester," Dawn mumbled under her breath, "because he's inside the gorilla cage."

Logan moved casually to stand in front of the gibbons. That gave him a clear shot of the action inside the cage. I remained on the other side of the primate enclosure, ready to shout for help, if necessary.

Suddenly, there was movement all around me. The bushes just outside the gorilla cage quivered. I couldn't see a face but I recognized a camping hat. Alan was in there, hiding.

The weird person in the jumpsuit and floppy hat moved swiftly past and around the corner of the primate enclosure. Claudia sprang forward from her position by the emu pen, snapping as many pictures as she could get.

"The gorillas!" Dawn cried. "They're escaping. What do we do?"

Alan sprang out of the bushes. "I'll head them off at the pass."

Logan ran for Alan. "Are you nuts? That male gorilla weighs four hundred pounds. He could crush you like a peanut."

Suddenly the side door of the primate enclosure burst open. Mr. Chester came running out in his janitor disguise, followed by the strange person in the jumpsuit, and the two gorillas.

"All right, Chester, freeze!" a female voice bellowed.

Mr. Chester stopped with one foot in the golf cart, and one out.

"Mike! Curtis!" the woman in the jumpsuit ordered. "Get him!"

Then a truly amazing thing happened. The two gorillas that had escaped out the side door of the primate enclosure stepped forward and grabbed Mr. Chester.

"What the — " Mr. Chester's words choked in his throat as the tallest ape removed his gorilla head.

"Wow!" Claudia sprang forward with her camera. "It's Mike in disguise!"

The other gorilla took off his head and shook his wet hair. Sweat was pouring down his face. "Whew," Curtis said. "It's like a sauna in here."

Then came the biggest surprise of all. The person in the coveralls removed her hat and sunglasses. "Well, Mr. Chester," Mrs. Wofsey said. "I see we've caught you red-handed."

"Wait a minute." Mr. Chester looked from the guys in gorilla suits to the now empty cage, and back to Mrs. Wofsey. "You haven't caught me doing anything."

Mrs. Wofsey turned to Claudia. "Did you get the shot of Mr. Chester leaving the gorilla cage standing open?"

Claudia nodded. "I got several pictures of that, plus a few of him putting on his disguise and taking the vet's golf cart. I got them all."

"Mr. Chester, with the help of these young people," Mrs. Wofsey said, "I can prove that you not only tried to set our gorillas free, but you also let the giraffe out of its corral and tried, unsuccessfully, to aid the gibbons in an escape. Now, you can deny it, and make this a long, drawn-out process. Or you can give me your resignation right now, along with a letter confessing your crimes and vowing never to work for any zoo or wildlife center again."

Mr. Chester's shoulders slumped. "It's not fair. I should have had that position. I put in fifteen years here. I was in line for it. The job was mine."

"I'm sorry you feel that way," Mrs. Wofsey said, signaling for Mike and Curtis to usher Mr. Chester over to the front office. "But I think these stunts prove that perhaps you really aren't cut out for a job like this."

We watched Mike and Curtis lead Mr. Chester away. Then Alan asked the question that all of us were dying to ask. "Where are Mojo and James?"

For the first time since we'd begun the stakeout, I saw Mrs. Wofsey smile. "Why, at the party, of course. They're the guests of honor. Early this morning Mike and Curtis moved them to the holding pen by the front office, making sure, of course, that Mr. Chester knew nothing about it. Then Mike and Curtis, being good sports, volunteered to take their places."

Dawn shook her head. "They really fooled me."

"That's because they made sure to keep themselves slightly obscured from the public," Mrs. Wofsey explained. "But you also must remember that Mike and Curtis have been working with and observing these animals for quite awhile. If anyone could imitate gorilla behavior, they could."

"Wow," Logan said. "I'm impressed."

158

"Instead of standing around here talking about the gorillas," Mrs. Wofsey said, "let's go see them. I would like to treat you all to a glass of gorilla punch and a giant piece of banana cake."

"*Before* or *after* the gorillas have had their pieces?" Logan asked, grinning slyly at Alan.

"Before, of course," Mrs. Wofsey replied.

"Whew!" Everyone sighed with relief.

Mrs. Wofsey shook her head. "I don't under — "

"It's a long story," Dawn said. "We'll explain at the party."

CHAPTER 15

"Alexander Kurtzman won the contest?" Claudia gasped. "But that's not fair. I mean, he is so uncreative. He carries that briefcase and is so, so — "

"Dull," I finished for her. We were sitting in Claudia's room, waiting for the Friday BSC meeting to start. "But he had Shawna Riverson on his team. She's certainly creative."

"Yeah," Kristy muttered. "I'll bet Shawna cheated and looked information up in the encyclopedia. How else would they be able to do a fifty-page report on the lions?"

"I wish Alan hadn't cheated," I murmured. "We had a good idea, and a cute title — Fins, Furs, and Flippers."

"But I thought we were only supposed to pick one animal and study it," Dawn said. "I mean, we only watched the gorillas — along with every other eighth-grader at SMS."

I waved one hand in the air. "It didn't matter anyway. After we found out that Alan had cheated on the emu, he confessed to cheating on the bears and seals, too. So we threw the whole thing out and studied Tigger."

"Tigger?" Kristy asked. "When did you do that?"

"All last weekend," Dawn answered for me. "Can you imagine having Alan Gray and Howie Johnson spend every second of the day watching you? I don't know if Tigger will ever recover."

I folded my arms stubbornly. "Well, it was the best I could do as a last-minute substitute project. Anyway, none of us won and none of us gets to go to Aqua World."

"Now just a minute," Kristy said, raising a finger. "I wouldn't say that nobody won. Did you see the newspaper this evening?" Kristy held up an article she had clipped from the paper. Mallory read the headline out loud. " 'Little Babar — free at last!' "

I clapped my hands together. "That's terrific news. When did it happen?"

Kristy scanned the article and said, "It seems that our Elephant Walk did a lot to raise money and interest in Babar's plight. A wealthy contributor stepped forward and, with his donation, plus the money we and the Free Babar campaign raised, there was enough to transport Babar to a new home."

"Where is he?" Dawn asked. "Can we go visit him?"

"This says he's going to be at a wildlife preserve in Sarasota, Florida," Kristy replied.

"That's a little far to ride our bikes," I kidded Dawn. "And I don't think the bus line stops there."

"Sarasota," Claudia mused, finishing off the last of the Oreos in her shoe box. "Warm and sunny. Just perfect for a little fellow from Africa."

Claud's clock changed from five-twenty-nine to five-thirty and Kristy officially called the meeting to order. But before we could even begin, Jessi suddenly bolted to her feet.

"Hey!" she cried. "I just thought of something. Remember when Matt asked Mojo who freed the emu, and Mojo made the sign for food?"

We all nodded expectantly. "Yes?"

"Well, Mojo might have meant Mr. Chester, since he was the one who always fed the gorillas."

"But Howie was the one who accidentally let the emu out of the cage," I pointed out.

"Oh," Jessi sat down again. "But I still think Mojo knew that Mr. Chester was rotten."

"Like the food," Claudia cracked. "Did you taste that banana cake at the gorilla party? It tasted like gorilla drool and really old bananas. Ew!"

That made everyone giggle.

Even though none of us won the trip to Aqua World, things weren't so bad after all. The Elephant Walk had been a success. And even though Kristy and Stacey hadn't spoken during the entire walkathon, they hadn't fought, either.

My group didn't win the extra credit but (miracle of miracles) we did get an A-. And so did Logan's group. I think it may have had something to do with the good word Mrs. Wofsey put in for all of us. She was extremely grateful for our help in catching Mr. Chester. To show her gratitude, she gave each of us — Logan, Dawn, Claudia, Howie, Alan, and me — lifetime passes to the Bedford Zoo.

So Logan and I are planning a trip to the zoo next weekend with Alan and Howie. Not!

About the Author

ANN M. MARTIN did *a lot* of baby-sitting when she was growing up in Princeton, New Jersey. She is a former editor of books for children, and was graduated from Smith College.

Ms. Martin lives in New York City with her cats, Mouse and Rosie. She likes ice cream and *I Love Lucy*; and she hates to cook.

Ann Martin's Apple Paperbacks include *Yours Turly, Shirley; Ten Kids, No Pets; With You and Without You; Bummer Summer;* and all the other books in the Baby-sitters Club series.

Look for #21

CLAUDIA AND THE RECIPE FOR DANGER

It happened pretty soon after we had started baking that day. Grace and Mari must have whipped up their recipe in no time flat and shoved it into the oven. I nudged Mary Anne when I noticed Grace setting the timer. *"They're* in a hurry, aren't they?" I whispered. "I think Mari rushes things, know what I mean?"

Mary Anne nodded, and both of us turned back to measuring and sifting. We had gotten to our station early that day, although we hadn't beaten Marty, Julie, Rachel, or Anna to the gym. (All of them must have showed up *super* early.) We set up our ingredients carefully again, and agreed that we would do our best not to leave our work station unwatched. Nobody was going to sabotage our recipe *that* day. We needed to make a good impression on the judges, and time was running out.

Anyway, there we were, following each step carefully. Shea had just turned on the oven to preheat it, when I first smelled smoke. "Shea!" I said, "is that *our* oven smoking?"

He opened the oven door, bent down, and gave a big sniff. "Nope," he said, shaking his head. "At least, I don't think so."

"Well, *something's* burning!" said Mary Anne. She put down the eggbeater she had been using and looked around. A few other heads popped up over nearby dividers, and I heard people asking each other what was burning. We were all sniffing and peering around, when suddenly, I heard Grace shriek.

"Fire!" she screamed. "Oh! Oh! Oh! Fire!" She was hopping around, waving her hands helplessly. "Help!" she yelled.

Read all the books
about **Mary Anne**
in the **Baby-sitters Club** series
by Ann M. Martin